Mauler

Shawn Williamson

HAYLOFT

First published 2005

Hayloft Publishing Ltd, Kirkby Stephen,
Cumbria, CA17 4DJ

tel: (017683) 42300
fax. (017683) 41568
e-mail: books@hayloft.org.uk
web: www.hayloft.org.uk

ISBN 1 904524 37 0

A catalogue record for this book is available
from the British Library

Papers used by Hayloft are natural, recyclable products made from wood
grown in sustainable forests. The manufacturing processes
conform to the environmental regulations of the country of origin.

Produced, printed and bound in the EU

I fear there is no doubt that this train of evil and its consequences originated in the infamous conduct of some of our countrymen.
Charles Darwin

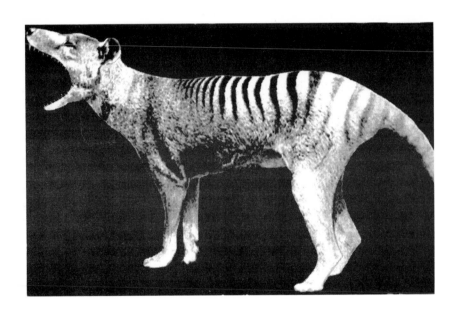

Drawing by Morgan Williamson

I would like to thank the following people for their support, moral and otherwise, during the course of writing this book: Dawn Robertson and Peter Koronka for believing in Mauler enough to publish it, Andrew Sinclair for being my teacher, critic and friend, Peter and Suzanne Greenhill for casting a critical eye over early drafts of the manuscript, Peter Davidson and Jane Stevenson for giving me some much needed advice about writing, Richard Freeman of the Centre for Fortean Zoology, CryptoCumbria and the Thylacine Museum for unwittingly inspiring the subject of this novel and helping me to get to know the thylacine, Patrick Gilbert, Maurice and Trish Hetherington, Doug and Liz Richardson, Richard Freeman of the Centre for Fortean Zoology, Ian Sinclair and Marcia Stephens for their encouragement and belief in me, Josefina de Vasconcellos and Morgan for being my scribe.

To my family and Andrew Sinclair

INTRODUCTION

What has been lost in modern literature is a sense of the elemental. Ken Tynan once wrote that, in all first novels, the hero is either Christ or Faust. In Mauler, the hero is the beast. Not since the writings of Jack London has there been a novel of such understanding of nature in the raw, and fierce liberty tempered by human compassion. The Tasmanian tiger, let loose on the Borders, is the mythical hero of Irish freedom, Cu'chulain. As it ranges free from its cage, it kills only for survival. Set against it are farmers and hunters, who must eliminate this threat to their flocks and herds. There can be no quarter. There can only be murder to the finish.

Setting this tale at the beginning of the 19th century, when rum and slavery were the chief trade of the Cumbrian ports, Shawn Williamson has returned to the bleak elements of the landscape. Himself a former sailor and boxer and monumental sculptor, he understands in stark prose the necessities of existence on the moors and the fells. His brilliance is to contrast the inhumanity of man, to man and to beast, with that rare light of non-conformist charity, which led to the end of the slave trade at that time. And to relate the killing of the tiger wolf on the Borders to the infamous Tasmanian Drive, when the islanders wiped out the Aborigines, was a touch of genius, in this wrenching story of ferocity and mercy.

This is a book that rends. In these words, the reader can almost smell the tearing of the flesh. And yet there is a strange beauty in the recognition of natural forces, whose power has been forgotten in our urban age. But in these pages, we lope and hide with the Mauler, we sense his hunger and his fear and his cunning. His only friend, the fell boy, is as wild as he, with an instinct for animals that makes him their eventual leader. He too must turn on man, the torturer, and the monstrosity of injustice. He must retaliate and suffer that injustice. He must redeem himself by the practice of what others preach but never do. And in the end, his spirit walks free with the tiger wolf to range the burns and the screes once more.

There is now a stirring and a recording in the Highlands and the Borders, and the Welsh mountains and Exmoor, of that struggle and bond between ourselves and those we hunt. That sense dates back ten thousand years to the times when we lived in small communities, surrounded by the wilderness. But then there was a common instinct between all living things, a mutual awareness described by another Williamson, Henry Williamson in *Tarka the Otter*. There was not only Edmund Burke's great chain of the living and the dead, but a feeling for the subtle and invisible strings that tied all animals together, who had to live and die in their creation and by their connection.

Mauler may track tall with the best work written of humanity trying to cope with the demands of nature. As with *White Fang*, the tiger wolf is raised as a freak and a gladiator, but in the marvels of his untamed being, he becomes a legend of retribution. Shawn Williamson has achieved that rare grace of modern times, a rebirth of history that illuminates the essential and eroding common country between beast and man.

Andrew Sinclair, May 2005.

Article in the *Cumbria Gazette*, 1 May 2005,
Girt Dog - The Return, by local correspondent, Mark Boswell.

If you look very carefully through a small window in the rear of Keswick Natural History Museum on a very bright day, you can make out the form of a remarkable exhibit. Although now faded and dusty and frozen in time in a glass display cabinet, you can clearly see stripes on its fur.

Upon closer examination, you might be forgiven for thinking that this creature was a cross between a tiger, a kangaroo and a wild dog. If you look closer still, you can see the neat criss-cross stitching that holds its skin together, and in some places the faint claret remnants of its own blood.

It is fixed in an attitude of controlled anguish, its huge head tilted tragically to one side, crouching low on its muscular legs amongst the fake flora and fauna of Australasia. Its erect moth-eaten ears are perked as if listening back through time to the sound of its tormentors. Its long cat-like tail, thick at its base and tapering towards its end, has been arranged in a position that could only have been contrived by man.

The specimen is particularly mysterious for two reasons. It is the largest example of the presumed extinct Tasmanian tiger ever recorded. Known in Cumberland as the Girt Dog, it was killed and its body recovered on Ennerdale Fell in 1810 - after it had decimated 300 sheep and run rings round the local hunts. How it got from Tasmania to Cumberland still confounds the experts to this day.

The second mystery is why the glass case containing the tiger wolf was broken into last night by thieves. Clippings were taken from the claws and hide of the beast and two of its teeth were removed. Some zoologists believe it to be composed from two specimens, the second having been used to patch up what was left of the Girt Dog. However, the Keswick Museum maintains that there is no evidence to support this theory. Ironically enough, this question might be resolved by testing the tiger wolf's DNA, the very thing that many believe the thieves were seeking. Roslin Institute, the creators of Dolly the Sheep, are already said to be involved in a rival bid with the Tasmanians to produce the first clone.

In the bigger scheme of things, nobody here seems to care who broke into the Keswick Natural History Museum or why. But perhaps we should care.

For if successfully cloned, the Tasmanian tiger (or Girt Dog to you) may stalk the fells of the Lake District once more.

1
CUMBERLAND, ENGLAND, 1810

A buzzard surveyed its kingdom, swirling in from the east and looking down on Ennerdale Fell. It called out its unmistakable and desolate cry as it soared over the fells and small lakes. A boy emerged through some bracken with a fox cub by his feet. The two had climbed half way up the fellside in search of rabbits. The boy had planned to stay on the moor for as long as possible, even all night. There was once a time when he would have snuggled under a warm blanket, protected from the elements, in a gypsy caravan.

Higher up, he could see two men finishing a length of dry stone wall. He recognised them straight away. They lived and worked on the fells in the summer. The boy knew that the work was not well paid, and he did not envy them toiling day in day out in all weathers for a pittance. They were packing their camp ready to head to the village, where the farmer would settle the account for their summer labours. The Fell Boy and his fox crouched low in the bracken. All the time he was studying the movements of the men at the stones. The fox cub had long since smelt them.

The wall-builders moved clumsily past, snapping twigs and crunching bracken underfoot. As they spoke, the Fell Boy strained to understand their broad Irish accents. The larger man had a cauliflower left ear and hands that looked like ham shank ends. His knuckles were caked in blood. As he stumbled past, the Fell Boy heard him mumble to his companion that he would butcher any prize-fighter, including Tom Cribb, within an inch of his life at Whitehaven. Then they could have as much ale and as many women as they wanted. The boy thought this was something he should see, for he knew of Tom Cribb, the champion of England. He was known to be solid and polite.

The two Irishmen blundered down the side of the hill like two giants in an insane asylum. When they were gone, the boy and the fox came out of hiding, with the sun already dropping behind the higher fells in the distance. In the twilight, boy and fox made their way up to where the men had been camped. They came upon the cinders of a fire with mutton bones littered about it.

While the fox cub sniffed the ground, the Fell Boy looked about. He noticed some metal objects glinting next to some rocks and reached down to pick them up. The smaller items were lead ball shot from matchlock pistols. They did not interest him, but the other things fixed his eyes as they glinted in the fading light. They were the most beautiful things he had ever seen. As he pawed the two gold crucifixes, his heart beat faster.

He became aware that he was being watched. When he looked up, he could see the buzzard circling the deep blue of the evening sky. Had it seen the gold? He turned to his fox cub, who looked back at his master as if to say, 'Leave it where it is. This could mean trouble - for you and me.' But the Fell Boy could not help himself, already taking up the crucifixes in his small dirty hand. He placed them carefully in the pocket of his leather breeches, knowing that the men would return, once they found out they had left their treasures. With the golden crucifixes stowed safe, the boy and the fox made their way even higher up the fell towards their secret cave.

LATER that night, the Fell Boy woke briefly. The light of the moon had been obscured by thick cloud. The fox cub had not slept most of the night, but it had managed to curl into the boy's warmth. Now they were both awake. Scratching sounds came from just outside the cave, as though some small creature was digging in the soil. The fox was nervous and had been for some time, but the boy calmed it down. He spoke softly to the cub under his breath and stroked its head. He felt almost certain that whatever was outside the cave posed no threat. Although he convinced himself that it must be a small creature, he could not get the fear of the wall-builders out of his head.

The boy thought about what to do next. He continued to stroke the cub softly with one hand and clutched the shiny crucifixes with his other. Then he prayed to the Faerie King – just as his family had done.

MUCH later in the night, the Irishmen were paying for their last round of ale at the Stone Dove. They were drunk and ready for their beds, when the prize-fighter asked his companion for the crucifixes. The wall-builders' stared one at the other, as if each man knew where the gold was and would lay it on the old oak table.

The landlady knew them, so she said, "Yea, lads, drink up yer ale an' git to yer rooms, for we are all tired." She meant it. She was used to dealing with ruffians and scoundrels, soldiers and tinkers. She could fire a pistol or use a fowling piece – even on a prize-fighter. The year before she had shot a bold ore miner, who tried to force himself on her and lived to tell the tale. The prize-fighter replied, "We will go no further 'til we find what's ours." He held out his brawny hand to his partner, expecting him to give up the missing gold.

The landlady warned, "Prize-fighter or no, O'Connor, five more minutes.

Or I'll throw ye to the floor meself. 'Tis late an' I want me bed."

O'Connor said nothing. Both men emptied the contents of their pockets on the table, a small heap of clay pipes, coins, snuff boxes, silver chains and phials of strong rubbing potions. But there was no sign of the gold. O'Connor was gutted when he realised that they had left their gold crucifixes on the fell. He was too proud to suspect that his mate would steal from him. They were thieves, and theft from each other would bring a rogue's end.

2

At first light, the buzzard circled round Ennerdale Fell where the boy and the fox were sleeping. It cried out with its pitiful cat-like call before heading west for the port of Whitehaven. It gained height and from below it looked like a small fly. Then it grew larger again, as it planed downward. Now the air was intense with cries. The buzzard avoided the screeching seagulls that swirled above the harbour, as busy as the hustle and bustle on the quay side. Merchant ships creaked and groaned in the swell and roll of the sea. Although the vessels were safely tied up alongside each other, there was still a sway. From ship to ship, the wood, masts and ropes all heaved as one.

One boat remained still and apart from the crush, its destiny different. She was the *Great Michael,* an armed merchantman and hunter of exotic animals, just returned from a year's voyaging. Her captain, Jacob Potter, was striding up and down the deck. He was gulping from a bottle of strong Whitehaven rum that had been steeped through wooden barrels until it was fire in the guts. His First Officer and brother-in-law, Mr Bibington, was struggling to keep up with him.

"Open the holds now an' position the cages on deck!" Potter barked to Mister Bibington. "The animals need air an' I need to see they're healthy! An' I hope to God ye've looked after them, whatever ye've got down there!" He took another swig of rum. "Anyways, I thought ye said ye were going to send the bo'sun to get Meg. I want that strumpet here." He looked up at the mainmast of the *Great Michael.* Taking a deep breath, he spat a great gob over the side of the ship with the prevailing wind. "Bo'sun!" he shouted, "break open the holds an' bring the cages an' animals onto the port side!"

Removing his cap, Bibington said, "I trust ye've paid off the constables an' customs an' excise, sir?"

Potter puffed himself into a great cockerel. "That's my concern, Bibington. Meanwhile, ye better give the hunters some time in Whitehaven. An' pay them."

A commotion erupted on board. As the crew manoeuvred blocks and tackles and swung ropes, they cursed and swore and stomped their bare feet upon the *Great Michael's* teak decks.

"Do ye want me to send one of the lads to get the circus train down here now, Cap'n?" Bibington asked. "An' maybe collect the animals as well, sir?"

14

"Aye, Bibington," replied the Captain, "there's riches to be made the morrow an' the town is bursting about its middle." He took another swig of the dark spirit. "I want a contingent of seamen by my side, all under arms. Make haste." He handed the empty bottle of rum to Bibington and, smirking to himself, went down to the dockside.

The Quaker Bibington looked at the bottle as though it were a piece of putrid flesh. But now the hunters were coming up from the hold. There were eight in all, proud trackers on hire from Ethiopia, slaves to none. They had captured the wild animals from the four corners of the earth. They understood little English, so they were guided by a group of squat British seamen with pasty white skin and bull necks. The hunters would need air and good grub with lime fruit to combat the scurvy. The seamen were charged to tend anything that would make money for Captain Potter.

The eight hunters were split into two groups of four and marched into Whitehaven. They trundled away from the *Great Michael* in single file.

"C'mon, lads, on the double!" The leading hand prodded the back of the last hunter and pointed towards some buildings stuck back from the harbour. They made their way towards the local inns and taverns, greyhounds herded by terriers. Standing in a small stone alcove on the quay side, the Captain merged into the red of the local sandstone, as if he could vanish at will. He watched the Africans wind their way along the dockside.

By now the banging and stomping had ceased on the deck of the *Great Michael*, while the ropes from the blocks and tackles were lowered into the hold. The men were yelling about the foul smell. A couple of old tars were sick over the starboard side of the vessel. The beasts in the cages below howled, bayed, barked, whimpered and screamed into the sea air now filling their prison. They were being brought out of the womb of the ship, as though being reborn.

The stench of the animals slowly wafted out from the *Great Michael* towards their new protector and guardian, Captain Potter, still skulking on the quay side and plotting his next move. The stink was caught first by dogs on the other ships, then by the dogs in the port. One hound after the other began to howl and bark, until the whole of Whitehaven was a chorus of baying. All over the harbour and beyond, hackles rose on the backs of men and beasts alike.

THE Fell Boy was on the move. Hours earlier, he and the fox had left their hideaway and were now descending the darker side of Ennerdale Fell. They were on their way to visit Farmer Thornthwaite and his wife, who lived at a nearby farmhouse on the other side of the valley. When the Fell Boy entered the farmyard, the farmer was already out. He was trimming the hooves and cleaning the feet of his Herdwick flock. The boy watched him until Thornthwaite looked up.

"Aye, well boy! Ye must've been up early this morn. Why d'ye wander so?"

The Fell Boy looked at the farmer and replied, "I'm making for the port of Whitehaven. I'm hoping to find a berth to the Americas. A safe place where I can take me fox." As the Fell Boy talked about his fox, his face softened and the tiny lines of worry and age on his young face disappeared.

"Well," the farmer said, "that fox is more like a pet dog. I wouldn't be surprised if some of them jack tars don't know the difference between a fox an' a dog in any case. If ye go in to the kitchen, me good wife has made some tatties an' eggs. She'll give ye some breakfast if ye ask nice. But leave foxy outside farmhouse."

The Fell Boy was looking to get a good meal, as his stomach had been rumbling with hunger throughout the dark night in the cave. He went in to the farmhouse kitchen through a carved stone doorway. There was a great wooden table. Sure enough there was food piled on plates ready for the workers coming in for breakfast. Mrs Thornthwaite was standing in the corner next to a small stove full of logs. She had ruddy cheeks and her hair was tied up in a bun, with a knitting needle of a pin keeping it all together.

"Well, boy, help yerself an' then be on yer way. We dinna want to be making a habit of this, ye know. If the poorhouse find' out we been helping ye..."

The Fell Boy made fists with his small hands. "I'm never going back there. I'll look for the same end as me family before they claim me back. An' when I've made me fortune, I'm coming back to avenge them."

Mrs Thornthwaite looked away. "Now there's no need for talk like that. There be's many a lad like you labouring an' pulling coal carts with chains under the sea at Whitehaven. So less of the feisty, ye wee Tartar."

The boy's fists tightened again and he clenched his tiny jaw. "Ye know who guards us. The Sinclair knights of Rosslyn Glen. I'll have them all back to fight for me. Them knights will come back. I say that."

"Well, me dear, what a fancy. Ye'll be telling me next ye're a prince ye be, or a king of some far country. Go on, away with ye."

The Fell Boy made for the table and bolted some eggs, potatoes, butter and bacon. He put a potato and a bit of bacon into one of his pockets for the fox and made for the door.

"Wait," said Mrs Thornthwaite. Cupping his face in her hand, she looked down at him fondly. Although he did not come often, he was like the son

16

she never had. "It were a damn shame about yer mammy an' daddy. Folks round here never did know the gypsy way. To hang a woman the way they did yer mammy, for they said she was a witch with the sight. Cruel it was, cruel."

A tear gathered in the Fell Boy's eye. "I know, I know," he said. "But me daddy died fighting for her. An' he took four of them gadgies to the grave with him." He sobbed, "An' when I'm back with the knights, we will have more."

As she stood at the door and watched him on his way, she muttered to herself, "Aye, them Gyptian Williamsons an' the rest of them, by God, the neighbourhood's settled without them."

"Hey, lad!" Farmer Thornthwaite was pinning down another Herdwick ewe into a wooden cradle and chopping at its hooves with a knife. He took a step back and felt his chin with his thick sausage fingers. "Aye, lad, if they come back the morrow in their pot carts, I'll sell them wool all ov'er again. Yer tribe, them Williamsons, were good uns. An' if ye ever want a job round the farm, come back some time."

Once clear of the farmhouse, the Fell Boy thought back to the pistols and ball shot he had seen in the kitchen. He had heard the story of how the farmer's father had been at the battle of Culloden and had fought for the King's Own Regiment, which had mustered further south at Lancaster. Sergeant Thornthwaite had brought back broad-swords and shields with spikes in them from that bloody battle. He was known for that in the Lakeland Fells.

Outside the yard on the small hedged path that led into the open fields, the Fell Boy decided to feed the fox with the food from the kitchen. But the fox was bolting and leaping around a hedge to catch a rabbit, grabbing hold of it before it had a chance to get into full jump. Taking the cony by the neck, the fox shook it like a puppet until it was dead. Then the fox brought the rabbit and laid it still twitching at its master's feet. The Fell Boy reached down and grasped hold of the rabbit's back legs, before the pair of them resumed their journey into the autumn light.

The Fell Boy was beginning to realise that his friend was no longer a cub. It had become a fully grown fox, independent of his influence and ready to return to the wild if it wanted. They carried on down the path towards the open fields.

O'CONNOR and his companion returned to their camp and started searching in a frenzy for their lost booty.

"By Jesus," O'Connor shouted, "we've been robbed. Robbed! Ye just know it when ye was robbed and we was robbed! If ever I find the person that's taken our booty, well then, I'll give him a hiding that, if it don't kill him, he'll beg me to finish him off!"

The smaller Irishman, Long, was crouching near the ashes of the fire. He had seen the footprint of a child. "Well, will ye look at this. We've a little pickpocket or a thief. Will ye take a look at this little footprint in these here ashes."

O'Connor rumbled over, his jugular vein throbbing and his face red with anger. "I'll murder the little bastard!" he yelled.

Long rummaged further up the fell and found the clues that would help him build a clear picture of the thief. This was his talent. O'Connor shifted uneasily from foot to foot, clenching his fists. The large jaw muscles under his ears rippled the skin of his face. Long had already worked out that the thief was a child, and from the footprints, it was most likely to be a boy. Long came back from the side of the fell. He had seen the cave, and so he guessed that the thief had stayed there overnight until first light before making for the nearest big town, perhaps Cockermouth or Whitehaven.

"Right", O'Connor said, "let's be on our way to Cockermouth to get some nags. If we have to, we'll ride him into the bracken."

3

Further away, an animal prison trundled down the steep cobbled roads of Whitehaven. The cages rattled on iron-rimmed wooden wheels. There were six carts with iron bars and an extra cart carrying manacles, chains and leather ropes. The driver and passenger wore breastplates of reinforced leather and copper helmets to protect them in case any beast broke out.

The townsfolk of Whitehaven stopped and stared at this curious procession of empty cages. Ladies in beautiful dresses and hats on high Parisian wigs held their hands to their mouths, as if the excitement would be too much for them. Their menfolk made forts around them, to console them in their fear. There was excitement all over by the time the people began to move towards the taverns and the gaming houses. Already some of the innkeepers had been alerted that the most famous bare knuckle fighter of the decade was making his way from Carlisle to offer a challenge to other lords of the ring. The prize-fighter's name was Tom Cribb. The local harlots were passing on the news to everybody who might pay them. The gossip cut through the town like a scythe through corn.

MEG Lowther had spent longer than usual making herself look beautiful. She had left the other whores and tried on a more demure look for her meeting with Captain Potter. She had given a sixpence to the cabin boy, who had told her that Potter was on the dockside. Flash and beautiful, she was taller than average, with a dark complexion and eyes of emerald green. Her mother had always boasted that she should be proud of her royal blood. She meant that she was a bastard of royal blood. She had her own room in the public house, the Capstan, but she longed for an easier existence, when she would be married and safe with a man of means, one who was rich and kind.

She opened her chest of clothes and precious belongings and pulled out a black scarf, which she fastened tight round her head. But Meg was shrewd, so she did not forget her ladies' pistol with the knife blade concealed in its handle. She took this away in her belt and covered it with a fold of her linen dress. She would tell all the scandal to Potter, including the news that the great prize-fighter Tom Cribb was on his way from Carlisle. She would add this as an enticement in her courtship, as she preferred to call it.

Meg took a side door into an alley, and she made her way carefully to the dockside. She did not want to turn an ankle on the cobbles. A gentle breeze was coming west from the harbour, carrying the fetid stench of animals from the hold of the *Great Michael*. She daubed some perfume under her nose to waylay the smell and pressed on towards the main dock.

Soon the darkness drew down. The handlers began to take the exotic animals from the hold of the vessel, to put them into the iron cages that had been left open and ready. The plan was that the Customs and Excise would turn a blind eye for two hours, while the animals and contraband were discharged from the vessel. This was part of the usual agreement between Captain Potter and the powers that were. The local constables would happen not to be in the neighbourhood, and the militia would be on the other side of the town.

As Meg approached the bows of the *Great Michael,* Captain Potter was smoking a cigar and drinking rum from a pewter tankard. He had set up a small table next to his ship, and he was standing with both arms outstretched, searching through some maps and papers. He had noticed Meg making her way along the dockside before she arrived. Yet he did not want to acknowledge her. The banging and drumming from the hold did not disturb him. Meg knew that the time she would spend with him this evening would be short. She could sense the excitement, not just at the docks, but in the whole of Whitehaven, over the arrival of the new beasts.

As she made her way down the harbour, she saw clusters of men clutching bull terriers that strained on woven leather leashes. She shuddered, knowing their purpose. The men were sizing up each other's dogs and bragging about their fighting prowess. Tomorrow the bets and the sport. The dogs and men slavered. When Meg reached Captain Potter, he turned on his heel to face her. His surly face dissolved into an awkward charm. He had not seen a woman for the last nine months, and for the last part of his journey, he had not stopped drinking rum. Now he put the bottle down on the table and bent his head forward, as though the muscles on his neck were no longer able to bear its weight.

Meg reached out to touch the side of his face, her hand as perfect as that of a statue of the Virgin Mary. All of the Captain's arrogance and bluff disappeared, and he was for a moment the person he used to be. In a soft low voice, as though he wanted no-one in the world to hear what he needed to say to her, he whispered, "Thank God ye've come to me." Then he reached into his coat pocket, brought out a bag of coins and handed it to her. This was his way. But for the first time in all the days that he had known her, she would not take it.

He took hold of her hand and pulled her towards him, burying his nose in the nape of her neck and breathing sodden breaths on her skin. For a moment, she was not in control. Mingled with the smell of rum was some other scent that drew her ever closer to him. As she felt the warmth of his breath, she looked at the stars in the evening sky. The sea had calmed, and all the ships in the Whitehaven basin were now still. The caged animals in the hold of the *Great Michael* were silent, although every now and again Meg could hear crashing sounds down below. Then the buzzard gently glided over the harbour, as silent as a sacred spirit. It spied the two lovers, their heads locked in the passion of the moment.

BY the time O'Connor and Long arrived at the Thornthwaite farm, the Fell Boy and the fox were long gone, making their way to Whitehaven. The thieves galloped into Farmer Thornthwaite's yard and struggled to pull up the old nags that they had picked up in Cockermouth. O'Connor dismounted clumsily, passing the reins of his mare to Long, who gripped them tightly. Farmer Thornthwaite owed the wall-builders three months' wages for the time they had been at their work on Ennerdale Fell. He had been expecting them and had prepared the payroll.

O'Connor blustered through the yard and banged on the farmer's door. "C'mon, Thornthwaite," he muttered under his breath, "we must be on our way."

Thornthwaite was already behind the door and opened it. He said to O'Connor, "Aye, aye, I have yer money here. Count it an' be on yer way. An' if ye want some more work next summer, then ye come back. Pleased to see ye've finished all the boundary walls for me flock." He saw the other wall-builder mounted in the yard. "Ye seem in a desperate hurry," he said. "Why are ye in such a race to be off?"

"Well, Jesus'll only know," replied O'Connor, "but we're after a small thief." As soon as he had said that, Thornthwaite thought of the Fell Boy. He went to the kitchen table, picked up a leather bag of coins and gave it quickly to O'Connor. "Thankee for that, Farmer Thornthwaite," said O'Connor, turning on his heel and going back into the yard.

Just as O'Connor was mounting his horse, the farmer said, "Now what would it be ye had stolen from ye?"

The two Irishmen looked at each other and said nothing. They turned their sorry mounts and clomped into the nearby lane. With his sharp eyesight, Long had seen rabbit guts and a skin close by. And pressed into the clay soil next to them was the clear footprint of a lad. Long halted his horse, lumbering out of the saddle and examining the mark as if he were a scout. Stuck in the footprint were the red brown hairs of a fox. Long took hold of O'Connor's stirrup and said to him, "I know what we're looking for. We're after a boy with a fox."

"Well, ye're a fine one," said O'Connor, looking down at Long. "Why didn't ye say that sooner?" O'Connor now knew that the thief had been to the farm. He would deal with the farmer later. "Right, let's get on." As they headed in the direction of Whitehaven, Farmer Thornthwaite released his trigger finger from his pistol. He would not need it now.

CLOSE to Whitehaven was a hill simply known to the Fell Boy as the Big Hill. At the bottom of the slope was a river. He had often stopped here to feed himself and the fox, before going into Whitehaven to beg, carry luggage, run errands or whatever work he could do. This time they only needed shelter, so they could cook the rabbit. The spot the Fell Boy had chosen was rich with trees and plants, a safe place in a brutal world. The river had a sense of rhythm and place. They rested under the green boughs, while he waited for the rabbit to cook on the fire.

The fox sniffed the air for trouble. Both beast and boy sensed that the town would be more secure, now that the sky was darkening. He would even risk seeing his friends, the circus people, one last time, before he went to find a ship in the harbour to take him and his fox red friend away.

After sharing the rabbit, the Fell Boy and his fox left the Big Hill for the last time to make their way towards the town. The palms of his hands and his top lip were sweaty with fear. In the woodland, the natural boundary of Whitehaven, the smell of the open countryside began to change. The aroma of fermenting rum and molasses filtered through the leaves, along with the stink of strong tobacco. But these smells could not disguise the stench of human cargo, the smell of black gelt, human slaves cramped together and chained in the cellars of some of the mansion houses of the port.

The Fell Boy moved cautiously through the trees. Every so often, the fox brushed against his leg, making him aware that it was by him. In the distance, he heard the growing drum of voices and laughter, as he approached the beginnings of the dirt roads that would lead him to the cobbled streets and his escape. The vessels in the harbour below were now in sight. Some of the ships' sails had not yet been stowed, and they flapped about like gutless handkerchieves from the spars. The canvas was glazed with light from the decks of the ships, where skeleton crews kept watch over their cargo.

Nobody saw the Fell Boy arrive in Whitehaven. Most of the houses had their front window boards closed firmly, although every so often he could see a finger of light through the joints in the shutters. Inside, ladies would be stitching needlepoint or reading the romantic visions of William Wordsworth, the more adventurous thumbing through anti-slavery journals, out of sight of their husbands. But further into the town itself, the hairs stood up on fox and child. There was a foreboding of danger in the atmosphere. The Fell Boy gripped one of the crucifixes, as though it bound him to the protection of his ancestors. He prayed that they would come back, and that the Faerie King on the cross would guard him that night and the next day.

The boy made a leash for his fox from an old leather belt. One thing that he had been taught to fear, through tall tales and myth, was the French. Cartoons showed them as anything from apes to dark and swarthy savages. Just recently, the Fell Boy had seen a drawing of a French spy that had been hung in the place where the black men were taken. He had laughed until his sides had split, because he knew the 'spy' to be only a monkey, just like the ones he had seen on the *Great Michael*. But the thought of seeing a real Frenchman frightened him.

His mind began to dwell on the plight of the black men in the cellars, who would soon be on their way to Newcastle across the desolate Cumbrian and Northumbrian moors. He wondered how the women of these big houses could sleep at nights, while below them the black gold moaned and shook and often died in their chains. He was free and bound only to looking after himself and his fox. He hoped that there would be a ship for him and his charge. He would have a chance to go somewhere far away from the savages that walked on their hind legs, wearing velvet britches and silken topcoats. Sometimes they had hair on their faces, sometimes they were bare, but always they were cold and cruel. Strutting about with their eyes looking upward, their heads perched on top of high collars, they might have been hung for some ghastly crime, their necks broken and their heads carelessly clicked back into place.

The Fell Boy had once witnessed a hanging. All the people had gathered around the victim. The criminal had twitched until he was dead, the people had then left, leaving their clay pipes behind them. Smoked during the man's dying, these lay scattered in a circle around his lifeless body. The pipe stems frightened the boy more than anything. They were like chewed bones spat out by those who had witnessed the end of a man.

4

Captain Potter was feeling good about his Meg, but what did the Greeks say! For one blessing, you get two curses. Propping his head on his hand, he looked at Meg asleep next to him in his cabin. Her dark hair swirled about her face on the pillows and over the Chinese satin sheets. He thought how serene she looked. The night was still early. He knew that he needed to get away from the vessel and what was in the hold. He climbed out of bed, dressed in his finest uniform and buckled on a pistol. Taking his quill and dipping it in dark blue ink, he wrote Meg a note:

Dearest Meg, I have gone to finish the business in Whitehaven. I will be back before sunrise. Please do not leave the vessel until my return. J.

Quietly closing the cabin door, he hastened amidships. At the gangway, a sleepy guard stepped quickly to one side as the Captain appeared. "Aye aye, sir," Potter heard, as he left the vessel and made his way along the dockside towards the pubs and brothels.

Potter's first stop was the Corinthian. He was sailing close to the wind and straight into hell. Slack faces stared up at him, drunk and high on laudanum. Wind-tanned and stubble-strong, they had escaped to the Happy Islands. The sailors threw their heads back in unnatural angles. Some wore old-fashioned tricorn hats and others sported red or blue handkerchiefs tied about their heads. A reek of strong tobacco from long clay pipes made a brown fog. The women had the masks of ghosts, their features hidden beneath white arsenic paste, set against blood red lips. They moved between the men and boys as if playing some macabre game of musical chairs. Up and down to the bar and back they went, banging down measures of ale in pewter vessels on to the oak tables, where loaded pistols and cutlasses were on show.

The Captain made his way to the back of the house, where he came across an old woman sitting astride a stool and chewing tobacco. She was the same as many cast as witches by the people around them. Potter could see her black leather boots, laced to six inches below her knee. There was no flesh left on her, but she seemed to be supported by more than muscle. Potter approached her with respect, sat down opposite her and took out some money from his waistcoat.

"I require some laudanum, ma'am," he said. She darted a look at him and recognised his features.

"Well," she replied, "ye come to the right place." She already had some prepared. Keeping one eye on the bar, she pulled a small bottle from between her withered breasts. Potter gave her a gold sovereign and said, "I will need more this weekend."

The babble from the pub calmed down. Two landlubbers approached Potter, taking off their hats as they did so. They had whiskers that grew down the sides of their faces, cut short at their jawbones. They were common working men, the backbone of Old England. If Britannia called, they would go.

"Captain, we have come to lay our bets." Potter looked up at them with glazed eyes. The old woman had already gone, slipping away as if through the cracks in the panelled walls.

"Good sirs", Potter said, "if ye knew what kind of dog I have in my hold, ye would see that your money is wasted. For I grant that no dog in this land shall best the creature I bring from Van Diemen's Land."

The men were not put out at all. "Well, sir", the taller of the two said, "we have game an' bigger bull terriers than ye've ever seen. We will wager three hundred guineas in a fight to the death with yer dog. This wager has the backing of Lady Dagobert herself."

"Sirs", Captain Potter said, "this dog belongs to no man. It has the stamp of Satan. And he is sent to me so he can show ye who is the true brute." At that moment, Potter was looking down on himself from the ceiling. He was not sure whether he or somebody else had uttered the words. The two men looked at each other. One of them offered Potter his hand to shake on the deal. Potter snapped back into reality. "The morrow then?" Potter said, alert again now and in control.

"I presume this match will be to the death," the taller man asked.

Captain Potter did not care, "I had a notion ye would say that."

"If ye wish, sir, the morrow it is. To the death. We shall pursue the occasion afore noon the morrow. We will have yer wager set by the sergeant-at-arms. And a constable. And they shall hold the purse."

Both men were now grinning to themselves. Captain Potter watched them merge into each other, as they moved out of the public house and into the night to prepare for tomorrow's dog fight. Both men thought that the Captain had lost his wits.

Some of the serving women sauntered over to Captain Potter. As sat there, drugged on his stool, they weighed up their prey, their dresses billowing over the huge heeled boots that kept them out of the filth of the road. Potter looked up as they approached, dazed as if he had seen two apparitions. Their white faces and blood lips betrayed nothing. "Well, if it ain't the great Cap'n Potter," sniped one of the ladies, while the other mockingly said, "Are ye going to have him or shall I? Looks like he's been on the laudanum. Easy meat. Grab him."

Potter recoiled abruptly, suddenly turning from sullen to angry in a second. "Keep yer distance, ladies", he growled, "I have this evening pledged my heart to yer madame. If she finds out ye flirt with me, ye'll get claws an' a madwoman's spit." The two ghosts stared at each other and then disappeared, blurring into the crowd. Off they went to sit at a table of drunken naval officers, who were in no fit state to uphold the King's peace on any sea, while the Captain slipped once again into an idle dream.

Then the light at the door grew dark, as though thunder blocked the small entrance. All heads turned as the first of the African hunters stooped to get into the house. They were quickly followed by another man, who had a neck as thick as the African's thigh, although he was much shorter than his charge. Hudson Israel, Whitehaven born and bred, was one of Captain Potter's best crew men.

"Alright, lad, there'll be time for singing later," Israel said. His beady eyes had already seen the dazed Captain sitting in the corner. "Ye can go and sit near him. Ye hear, Suniman?"

The huge Ethopian nodded insolently. Suniman was followed by the other African hunters, who all had to stoop low to get through the door into the tight fug of the Corinthian tavern. Soon they were all gathered around the Captain, who liked their exotic company. The other seamen from the *Great Michael* had loosened up under the influence of spirits and ale, and were now mingling freely with the rest of the house. They moved differently from the Ethiopians, less of the greyhound, more of the terrier, purposeful and inquisitive.

Israel was in deep conversation with his captain. "I done everything ye say, sir. Beastie's well fed with best meat I can find." He lowered his voice until it was barely audible. "But my God, sir, there's something strange about this creature. He don't notice us at all. Just pacing and panting and every so often letting out a single bark that makes yer spine crawl. I swear to God, sir, one morn I goes down in the hold to change the animal's water and I couldn't tell what manner of creature it was. 'Tis all creation and none at all. We have some fierce ones down there, but I grant, sir, none of the other beasts can abide that creature. The other thing is, sir, the hunters say our beastie gave itself up to them... as if it meant to."

Potter looked intrigued. "Well, Hudson, I know not what it is or why it is here, but we shall see what it is made of on the morrow when it meets the fighting dogs. And if I win five hundred guineas at the first event, I promise ye fifty of those guineas for yerself. If we lose, then ye shall sail with me another time, but no pay for six months. Done?"

"Aye, aye, sir," Israel said.

BY the Corinthian was the Royal Signal. In this house the performers of the menagerie and the Scarlet Circus were gathered. Standing in the middle on a table was a stocky dwarf. "Well, my little beauties," he declared, "once again we stand... on the day... before the great spectacle and feast of September the seventeenth. Be proud of this day, because it is a day... when we jacks... we royal high uglinesses... RULE THE BLOODY ROOST!" There were loud cheers from the fifty odd performers that formed a circle around their spokesman and elder. They were every shape and size, but they all had one thing in common. They were despised by other people for most of the year and loved by them during festival time.

Grouped on the outside, and drinking heavily, were the menagerie cage drivers. Some were so mutilated by war and naval battle, that they were seen as cripples instead of heroes. Yet the great Captain Potter had seen a use for them. Their masks and body armour lay in a heap on another table. Then a tall woman with a Cleopatra headpiece swayed through the crowd and stood before the dwarf. Her beauty hushed the folk around the table. In one swift gesture, she threw down her cloak. From the waist up, she was naked, except for what looked like shining patterns of soot on her skin.

She cried, "Now, my people, imagine how much pain I went through getting these tattoos and blackening my body? Do you think I wanted them? I could have been the Queen." There was a strange beauty in the tightly-packed pictures of snakes, dragons and demons etched into her body and over her breasts. "But I am still Sheba, Queen of Egypt! And princess of the East!" At that she covered herself and the crowd cheered and laughed.

The dwarf opened his arms, took a flying leap and launched himself at a huge onlooker, who caught him. The circus strongman placed him carefully on the ground and then twirled his huge curly moustache. He grinned, "Petch, good to see you."

"Renaldo! My friend!" the dwarf replied.

OUTSIDE the Royal Signal, the fox alerted the Fell Boy, but it was too late. For a brief moment, the boy thought his time had come. He was wrestled to the floor and his fox snatched from him, the leather leash ripped from his small hand with ease. However much he struggled, the boy could not get free. Someone sat astride his chest, pinning him to the ground with hideous strength. His heart beat fast and his fox squealed in the shadows. The Fell

Boy looked up to see the face of his friend Pert. He sighed, as his fear turned to relief.

"Well, if it isn't our young friend!" Pert said. "Don't you worry, my boy, you're in good company. We are the children of the Scarlet Circus – and luckily for you that is too."

The dwarfs laughed, pulling the Fell Boy to his feet, patting him hard on the back and dancing round him holding hands. They were all smaller, but considerably broader than the Fell Boy. His heart was beginning to slow down again, as his fox was given back to him, and Pert placed its leash back in his hand. The three dwarfs gambled around the Fell Boy, singing:

> A ring a ring a roses
> a pocket full of poses
> a tishoo a tishoo
> they all fall down

"Come with us, come and have a meal," Pert said. "There is someone who wants to talk to you."

"I am so lucky," the boy said, "to meet me friends this great night. But look at me, all cold and wet. I need grub. And some meat for me fox."

"Then a horse sheep you shall eat, boy!"

Now the group set off down the hill to where the rest of the Scarlet Circus were. As they drew closer to the Corinthian, the Fell Boy's heart beat faster, for he knew that he was nearing his goal. He looked up at the stars, the sky bright in the light of a full moon. "Is there a ship bound for the far end of the world?" he asked.

There was no answer, but one of the dwarfs pointed to a lookout tower by the houses of the gentry, and the group rattled on down the cobbled road. The great bells of St James' Church sounded eight chimes. A salute of guns was fired from the harbour and a galaxy of fireworks lit up the sky. Scuttling down to the church's wrought iron gates, the verger was locking them hastily, bundling the key into his pocket and sidling back inside the building to fasten the doors. The Fell boy could hear murmuring and cheering coming from all the public houses. Squeals, guffaws, coughing and curses were jackdaws in the air. The beacons in the harbour were being lit, casting red and yellow monsters and serpents on the dark sea swell. Somebody fired his pistol at the man in the moon, while others pretended to wrestle the weapon from him in mock combat, like silhouettes in a Chinese puppet show.

Now the iron cages were making their way towards the *Great Michael*. The colossal horses drawing them wore heavy blinkers, so that they would not be distracted in their task. The cage guards and draymen were kitted in their body armour, while bright torches of burning bitumen were tied to the bars. They rumbled over the cobbles as a fire-breathing dragon.

The Fell Boy was sick in a fit of nausea and fear. He coughed and spluttered, while his dwarf friends laughed and clapped their hands on his back. "Ye see," Pert shouted, grasping the Fell Boy's shoulder, "the cages are on their way to collect the beasts. Tonight we shall eat, drink and feast. For the next two days, we shall be the kings of Whitehaven."

The town had erupted. Men and women danced in and out of doorways. Wicker lights were lit in upper windows and crying children, frightened by the noise of the evening, were given rum and sugar to quieten them. And above, on the grand terraces in their marble halls, the gentry stood back above it all.

CAPTAIN Potter followed the iron cages down to his vessel. Holding his hands tightly behind his back, he strode forward like a man in mourning at his own funeral. He was dwelling on the beasts he had in his possession, in particular the one he was expecting to make him a considerable fortune. The noise from the hold was drowned by the ecstatic shouts and screams of the folk around the harbour, as if in a feast to the god Pan. As the iron caravan came to a halt, Captain Potter marched past the cages and shouted at the foc'sle deck of the *Great Michael,* "Haul the beasts out of the hold! Now!"

There was a harsh clank of metal hooks on iron bars. The frightened menagerie barked, yelped, hissed and growled from below deck. The first cage in the hold held a sleek black panther as big as a tiger. Its eyes were small pits of fire in a black fathomless head. It snarled, its mouth opening to expose a scarlet tongue framed with huge ivory fangs. It tore at the air with a paw, making the merchant sailors jump away.

"C'mon, lads, have him down here and loaded!" shouted the Captain. He could hardly hear a whisper of "Aye, aye, Cap'n" from the decks. But soon the panther's cage was dropped the final three feet onto the dockside, the big cat mad with fury spitting furiously. The cage driver guards, checking their body armour and face guards, unlocked the doors of one of the cages on wheels. They prodded the panther with a large wooden hook, forcing it from its sea cage to its new one on land.

"Bo'sun!" the Captain barked at the top of his voice, "I want this animal fed. And I want the lambs butchered - or why not just feed it one alive! And leave the monsters till last!" He paced about maniacally. "I can see them now, bo'sun! The Baboon-faced Lady and Monkey Girl, now there's a treat for the Prince's eye!"

Potter's strutting and shouting was upsetting Meg, who was watching from the window porthole of the captain's cabin. Suddenly he threw his hat into the air. "My God, I have it!" he bellowed. "Bo'sun, feed the two-headed sheep to the panther the morrow! The townies will love it!" His triumph was washed down and he felt he needed another dose of laudanum. The Captain was now back in total control, and his performance on the harbour had driven Meg to tears. She clenched the handrail of the foc'sle deck, from time to time bringing her handkerchief out of her cuff and holding it to her face. More strange sounds burst from the hold, as a cage crammed full of screeching monkeys was hoisted from below. They clambered about the bars, pulling and tugging at them, as they chattered and screamed.

"Aye, that's right, get them into the cages!" the Captain yelled. The magnificent dray horses that had been hand-chosen to pull the cages stood silent, as though cast in bronze, their blinkered heads lowered close to the ground. Another cage emerged from the hold, draped in a flag of the Red Ensign. It was dumped near the others being loaded onto the menagerie train.

"Ah, here we have the pride of the fleet!" Potter joked. "I want the flag tied tight to the side of the cage. No-one must see the beast until tomorrow." But he could not resist moving closer to the cage and peering in. Although he knew what was inside, he still drew a sharp intake of breath, and he felt every hair on his body stir.

"My God," he whispered under his breath, "it has no fear!" The creature was glaring in defiance at his captor. The Captain quickly let the flag fall back over the cage, before anyone else had the chance to inspect the beast. "Say nothing," he hissed, turning towards the small crowd gathered around him. As he strode past the monkeys' cage towards the *Great Michael*, the apes tried to pull at him through their bars. He struck at them with his riding crop. "Get back, ye fiends! You're no better than the townies!"

The African hunters were now returning along the dockside, loose and relaxed. They laughed and spoke to each other in their own language, steering well clear of the creatures in the cages.

"C'mon, lads, I want ye well rested for the morrow. and I want ye in yer best bull hide. Shields and spears and all!" Hudson Israel was shouting like a drill sergeant. One of the hunters put his hand on Israel's shoulder and smiled.

5

By first light, the prize ring had been set up. A stout rope was set around four huge stakes hammered into the ground, their perimeter twenty-four feet, the standard measurement for a prize fight. Tom Cribb in his might stood in one corner, backed by his squad of seconds and some London ruffians. The whole town had come to the fight scene, packing into the small market square to see the master prize-fighter at work. Well-dressed women, standing by the sides of husbands or lovers, waited eagerly for the match to begin.

A line was drawn in the sand and the seconds brought the two combatants to the mark. The contender was a huge tinker. The fight master announced, "And your consideration, please, for Mister Joshua Farr!" The great Cribb needed no introduction.

Both men stepped up to the scratch in the sand, and the fight began. Farr went all out to batter his opponent, but Cribb was a master of defence and milled on the retreat, leaving the well-muscled Joshua Farr punching the air where Cribb had once been. The crowd roared its appreciation. Many of them, who were now drinking gin from silver flasks, were cheering the champion. The womenfolk, rich and poor alike, turned away for fear of the sight of blood.

The courage of Joshua Farr could not be turned. He moved ever closer to the elusive Cribb, hitting out with his chop fists. This created consternation among the many who had laid their bets in Cribb's favour. Both gladiators took to clubbing and jabbing at close quarters. The tinker showed no pain, and for this the champion punished him severely. His teeth rattled, after Cribb hit him upon the jaw with a left-handed blow. The crowd were by now slack in the face. Farr's backers looked heavenward as if expecting a divine miracle from the skies.

When his seconds ushered him out for Round Five, the tinker was thundering and lunging. Yet he rallied to bore his opponent to all corners of the ring, shouted on by the heroes in the crowd clinging to the ropes.

The contest was marred in Round Six by Farr's family. Seeing their son was in trouble, they moved closer to the ropes to curse and spit at Cribb. The mob answered with boos of indignation and derisive laughter. Farr took hold of Cribb and dumped him on the floor, inciting the crowd to fury. Cribb had now taken the worst his opponent could throw at him. He rose to one knee to take his count. Spying the huge frame glistening above him, Cribb levered himself up from the sand and hit his man with a left blow to the slats. This time it was the tinker that fell, the wind slapped out of him.

Showing the honour and courtesy for which he was famous, Cribb backed off gently, allowing the contender to rise in his own time. The crowd cheered in this spectacle of fair play, further enraging Joshua Farr, who rose and rushed at his tormentor. But with a coolness and confidence that did Old Albion justice that day, Cribb side-stepped and punched to Farr's head, closing one of the tinker's eyes and causing a terrible swelling to his cheek. Although his punishment was dreadful, Farr did not go down. Rallying and now truly frantic, he began to rain low blows onto Cribb's midriff, offering Cribb the opportunity to sneer. Pinned into the corner by the tinker, the champion took further blows on his arms, before he unexpectedly turned the tide, giving the tinker the worst drubbing of his life, hit after hit to his jaw. The tinker gave way, out of his senses.

Now Cribb finished his man, felling him with a right hand that would have levelled an ox. He held his fist up in the air, as he was joined by his bottle-holder. Both men danced a slow mock Scottish jig. That was it. The tinker's family stormed the ring to square up to Cribb and his gang of London ruffians.

Now a drama took over from the prize fight. Some young actors made a timely entrance into the ring, all dressed in theatre costumes. So Samson slew the Philistine with the jaw bone of an ass, Cain pierced his brother Abel with a spear, Ajax defied the lightning, and a gladiatorial fight broke out. Finally, Hercules struggled with a lad wearing the hide of some unfortunate creature of the jungle, his face painted as a lion. The contender was carried away from the ring by his family, and the mock battle ended to cheers from the crowd.

BY the time Captain Potter arrived on the scene, Tom Cribb had already defeated three other hopefuls, none of whom had laid a mark on the champion's features. Captain Potter was dressed in his very finest American style naval uniform. He had timed his arrival perfectly. Although he had shaved, there was no concealing his fatigue, but he was fuelled by laudanum. Yet he leapt nimbly onto a box that had been set up for him by some of his men. He looked across to the crowd, who were waiting for the next fight. More and more people drifted into the market square from the surrounding streets and the taverns and parlours of Whitehaven.

"Your attention, please, my lords, ladies and gentlemen!" the Captain announced. The crowd grew quieter and looked in his direction. "Today I shall show you a battle that shall long be remembered on these shores! For

I have a CREATURE... the likes of which has NEVER been seen before by the human eye!"

The crowd, now thickening, murmured with delight. People were holding handkerchieves over their faces to disguise the smells of other folk.

"This creature from HADES I wager today... a vast fortune on its prowess in the canine arena. And my beast will ONLY fight to the DEATH!"

A further rustle of wonder vibrated through the crowd. By now some stared open-mouthed, in horror at what the showman was saying.

"Yes, my friends," he continued, relishing the reaction of the crowd, "this creature is TRULY diabolical... And I wager here today, Captain Potter's pledge... FIVE THOUSAND GUINEAS... for any dog that can despatch this canine wonder before the day is out! Ladies and gentlemen - I give you - CU'CHULAIN!"

ALREADY the fighting dogs gathered in the area were being brought to the pit, dug by the crew of the *Great Michael*. And near Market Square, the Fell Boy was making a farthing here and a penny there, carrying bags and helping rich ladies in and out of carriages. "Thankee, me lady," he would say every time he opened the hansom door to hold out his arm for some rich dowager on her way down. They tipped him well, and quite soon he was buying his own meat from the Royal Signal, like his friends from the Scarlet Circus. He had left the fox with one of the dwarfs, now feeding it scraps from the last evening's feast.

Captain Potter waved from his box to the lookout stationed on the main mast of the *Great Michael*. The menagerie rolled and cranked its way along the quay side with its sorry cargo. All the cages were covered with Union Jacks, the corners held either by dwarfs or the mutilated disfigured guards. As the Scarlet Circus entered Market Square, there was an uproar from the gathering. Captain Potter tried to quieten the crowd by raising and lowering his hands like some ghastly puppeteer. "My friends today you shall see WONDERS from around the WORLD which will both AMAZE and REPULSE you!"

A sudden explosion spouted a puff of black smoke. Out of the grime appeared the woman with tattoos all over her body. Captain Potter removed his top Hornblower hat and doffed it in the direction of his first exhibit. "From the land of the Pharaohs, I offer you - the Queen of Egypt, the AMAZING PAINTED LADY!"

The crowds cheered again and the Queen of Egypt bowed low. She then stood upright and gingerly parted her mantle from the waist up. The crowd gasped. The ladies in the audience pretended to turn away, but they were sneakily curious, some peeping from behind handkerchieves as their men-folk gaped at the emblems on her breasts. Some of the local harlots laughed and slapped each other on the back. Although naked from the waist up, the Queen of Egypt seemed to wear an intricate lace garment of snakes, beetles, pyramids, stars and monsters. In a loud and dignified voice she declared, "Am I not the Queen of Egypt, descended from the Great Pharaoh himself, returned to walk among you for a brief moment. I have heard of the generosity of the English. So please, fill my purse with your silver, and you shall be forever lucky. Make a wish if you will." She threw her arms above her head to further extend her tattooed breasts, while coins were thrown at her feet.

A man shouted from the crowd, "I would like to see what ye got painted on yer arse!" And the whole crowd burst into an uproar of laughter. Once it had died down, the Queen of Egypt coolly replied, "I would like to see what you've got in your skull!" This sally led to cheers, and the multitude joined in mocking the man.

Before further insults could incite them, two dwarfs jumped in front of the Queen of Egypt. They acted their clown routines and did their mock acrobatics, while she disappeared. Another two dwarfs pushed back the spectators to erect a makeshift circle. The first two slapped each other round the back of the head, fell to the floor and rolled around in a ball. Another began juggling devil sticks, which had the crowd in more fits of laughter, while his partner did the talking.

"I have here a gifted swine that can see the future! Tis Porgy the Pig with the second sight." The other pair of dwarfs reappeared with a small pig, which they guided into the circle stage with a stick. The squealing pig was decorated with crescent moons and the signs of the Zodiac. The speaker continued, "This is the very same seer that prophesied for our illustrious poet, that son of Cumberland, Mister William Wordsworth."

The pig was lightly whacked with a cane on its rear end, causing it to skitter round, its trotters rattling on the boards. It halted suddenly. "Ah, we have a message, patrons!" the dwarf speaker announced. He bent down and picked up one of several parchments pinned to the outside of the circle. Like a town crier, he opened it and began to read it out. "The devil dog shall taste victory in the pits!"

The crowd wailed and booed. The dwarf silenced them by proclaiming, "This is the work of the prophesying pig. Take heed, my friends. And for another penny, he will guide you on the odds of your wagers."

Despite the heated activity in the centre of Market Square, the eye of Captain Potter came to rest on the Fell Boy, who was looking straight at him.

So the child did not see the huge hand that gripped the top of his head. It was the grasp of a maniac with the strength of three men. His skull would surely crack and be crushed.

"Right, ye little bastard," the man hissed. "It's time for ye to meet yer maker." The Fell Boy knew the voice of the big Irishman. "Gimme's back the gold – gimme me back what's mine and I'll spare ye."

The Fell Boy froze with fear. Before he had time to dodge, the Irishman had clubbed him to the ground with one swipe of his huge right hand. Nobody took any notice of the sprawling child. The lady in the carriage that he had been attending simply stepped over him. But he leapt up and yelled at the top of his voice, "I'll scupper ye, sink ye down!"

The angry Irishman picked the boy up by his shirt and held him off the ground with his legs kicking the air. "Right, ye little game chicken, empty yer pockets or I'll gouge yer eyes out and feed ye to the lion."

The Fell Boy kicked and jibed, "Why don't ye fight with Tom Cribb, ye great blockhead!"

"Well, boy, that's already been arranged - after I've had ye chops for breakfast."

Captain Potter jumped down off his box in the middle of the square and strode over to see what was going on. "Sir," he interrupted, "what's yer business with this little wretch that you should hang him by his shirt?"

"That'll be none of yer business, sir," the Irishman said, "but this little varmint stole two very precious things from me."

"Well, let's see," the Captain said. "Turn out your pockets, boy." The Irishman released his grip and the boy fell to the floor in a heap.

By now, Cribb had seen the Irishman and walked across to him. "Well, if it ain't old Jo O'Connor," he said.

"Well, Tom," O'Connor said, "I've come today to challenge ye and to oblige a friend, 'tis me will fight ye. But first I have business here - I want me gold."

The boy was now turning out his pockets and the two gold crucifixes tumbled out. He whimpered, "I'm protecting the Faerie King on the cross from 'this brute."

The Captain looked at the Fell Boy and then at O'Connor and said, "Well, sir, you can see that the boy does not know the significance of what he's taken." Then he stared right into the eyes of O'Connor and said, "And if you could tell me, sir, where you got these trinkets, for it appears you are not a rich man. And you are most certainly not a priest."

For a moment, O'Connor was put off balance. The penetrating gaze of Captain Potter would have opened up a window in his soul, if he had one.

"Perhaps you would care to wager the gold in the dog pit later." Potter sneered, "but then maybe you're not a betting man, sir." The Captain bent down in front of the dumbstruck Irishman and picked up the crosses. "I trust that's a wager then? Five hundred guineas against your crosses. Meanwhile, I shall entrust them to the local magistrate. He shall hold them until the wager is done."

The Irishman was furious and pulled back a fist, as if he were about to strike the Captain between the eyes. But Tom Cribb had now grasped his bent arm in an uncomfortable twist. "There will be time enough for that with me, Jo lad, so let's get ready for fighting."

The Fell Boy looked at Captain Potter and said, "I was hoping to get a berth as a cabin boy on any ship for foreign lands. The Faerie King was looking after me, I know that." His eyes welled up. The Captain looked at the boy sadly, "Well, lad, we might just be able to look after ye somehow." The Fell Boy, fearful now that he had lost his Faerie King, darted off. He side-stepped through the crowd, past the coaches and across the cobbles to the Royal Signal.

THE main contest, between Tom Cribb and Jo O'Connor, had begun. The crowds had increased by several hundred in a short space of time. Many came to offer their support to the heroic champion of old Albion. For this fight, the Fell Boy had shimmied up a cast iron gaslight protruding from a monument to the West Cumbrian men who had fought the Jacobites at Culloden. He sat on the arm of the gaslight, his frail figure swaying in the prevailing wind. He could see his tormentor, O'Connor, limbering up, stripped to his dirty cotton long johns, which were supported by a thick brown belt. The Irishman was neither well-muscled nor fat, but something in between, which betrayed his real strength. He had a bald oversized head that sat on his shoulders like a pumpkin. Cribb, in comparison, was smaller and not as heavily marked. To the Fell boy he looked as if he could have been the Irishman's son.

"Begorra, Tom Cribb," O'Connor said, "ye may well be champion at this time, but I have two fists that'll make me champion." And he held up his fists and declared, "Mother drums an instant death." Cribb marched up to the scratch in the sand, with his fists raised quite calmly, in contrast to the Irishman, who charged at it. He always bore a grudge against anyone who slighted him. Before he had a chance to lay into the challenger, Cribb glanced towards the animal pits, distracted by the start of the first dog fight of the day. Loud cheers could be heard, and the occasional monstrous bark from the pit itself. For this side glance, Cribb paid dearly. Seizing his opportunity, O'Connor swung a roundhouse right, which not only knocked Cribb over, but took out two of his front teeth. The Irishman stood back as Cribb staggered to his feet, spitting blood. "Well, Tom, I think we're even, lad. Now c'mon, let's have a clean fight." There was a loud booing from the crowd, and militia men moved closer to the ropes, to stop any foul play.

The Fell boy's grip on the iron gaslight tightened, as he watched Cribb brace himself for the next onslaught. O'Connor charged again, aiming a huge overhand right at Cribb's head. Cribb sidestepped and began milling on the retreat. The Irishman blundered back, while Cribb, springing off his back foot, unleashed a barrage of punches to the guts of the contender. As O'Connor doubled over, the wind could be heard gasping from his stomach. And so it went on, the Irishman attacking and the champion defending, with Cribb's hits and punches slowly wearing his adversary down.

By the end of Round Three, it seemed that O'Connor was losing his marbles as well as his wind. But in the next round, to the astonishment of every spectator, O'Connor rallied with enough strength to grapple with Cribb. He held the champion, lifting him high into the air and throwing him to the ground with a dull thud. In its severity, this fall took some of the senses out of Cribb. Seeing that the Irishman had got the upper hand, many cheered, and the betting turned against the champion at high odds.

Cribb staggered to his feet. He was noted for being able to take punishment in the extreme, but then he showed his true mettle. He endeavoured to close the Irishman's eyes, but the persistent contender warded off such blows with uncommon neatness. But in Round Five, the champion levelled O'Connor to his knees. He moved to the mark and waited for the Irishman to rise. After dealing further punishment to O'Connor's head, he gathered his wind and inflicted upon the contender a horrible drubbing, turning his head into a bloodied turnip. The Irishman's seconds and bottle holder jumped into the ring and guided him to his stool.

The Irishman began Round Six lurching to his feet, on rubber legs, as though drunk. On setting to, he planted a blow over Cribb's guard that did little damage. Shifting to one side, the champion returned the compliment with a blow to the Irishman's already disfigured ear, causing him to cry out in pain. Still determined to do his best, O'Connor aimed a hit at Cribb's throat, but it glanced off his sweaty neck. The champion dropped his weight slightly, and upped a punch to the Irishman's solar plexus, bringing him to all fours. Both Connor's eyes were closed and he could barely see.

Cribb's true nature was shining forth. His dander was up. Had the crowd not known him better, he looked as if he was about to punch the Irishman as he was down. Cribb moved to the scratch and said coldly, "Yer peepers are blind, Jo. Would ye care to make the scratch so I may finish yae and make yea oblivious to yer shame?" Before the Irishman had a chance to reply, his second and bottle-holder threw the towel onto the claret-splattered sand. "Well, Jo," Cribb continued, "ye nearly had me, lad. 'Tis a pity ye can't see whether ye'll win the five thousand guineas on the dog fight."

O'Connor replied in a low voice, "Well, as long as I can hear, I've got some hope. But mind ye, Tom, I'll expect ye to offer me the hospitality of another challenge next year."

6

The Fell Boy could hear the arrival of the menagerie caravan. The iron-clad wheels had been bound with leather to muffle their rattle. All hands of the Scarlet Circus began to take down the flags draped over the exhibits. The crowds surged towards the cages in a pell mell rush, so that anybody in front was thrown to the ground under the weight of the crowd behind. Instead of helping the victims to their feet, the crowds trampled them. Young and old alike, they were left to crawl away or lie as they were.

The first exhibit to be unveiled was a melancholy two-headed goat, complete with four horns and four eyes. The animal was bucking at the huge crowd that had come to see it. Captain Potter was there too, climbing up the iron ladder on to the top of the cage, where he began the first of his diabolical sermons in his flowery showman's style.

"Deep from the desert, after much adventure and exploration, we found this OBSCENE animal, the spawn of a licentious act between a goat and a ram. It is, of course, tes-ti-mony to the vile nature of the black continent, where other horrors of nature are in ABUNDANCE!" The crowd recoiled while some people threw their hands up in the air, as if to plea for an explanation from the Almighty. Captain Potter jumped down from the top of the cage and ordered the exhibit to be covered again, now that it had achieved the desired effect.

All attention was fixed on the second cage, as its flag was removed to expose, if it were really so, a unicorn. This time Potter addressed the crowd from the ground. "Silence, please!" he bellowed and rolled his eyes. "Further down from the mysterious black continent we came upon a small island where a snow white princess was looking after this unicorn. And she pleaded with me to look after it - to take it into my care - and give others the opportunity to see this mythical creature." Sure enough, the white pony had a horn growing from its head. It was a foot and a half long. "NOW, my friends, shavings from this horn, if ground into a paste and taken with Dr Todd's famous herbal remedy, will restore the carnal desire of the uninterested male. The potion will be on sale at the end of the carnival. For just one guinea, gentlemen, guaranteed to keep your woman from straying."

There was burracking from the crowd, some laughter and feigned shyness from the ladies, although a tart shouted, "Why don't ye take some of' it then, Cap'n Potter? Ye eunuch!"

The Captain was angered and, for once, speechless. He got hold of one of the circus dwarfs and snarled in his face so that nobody else could hear. "I want you to seek out that bitch and toss her into the harbour." Then regaining his composure, he shouted, "Now, ladies and gentlemen, there will be enough of this unicorn horn to go around for all! And if you are the size of my friend here, then it will go twice as far! Now perhaps you would like your fortunes told. But not by a gypsy."

More people were filtering in from the streets of Whitehaven, but they were moving in the direction of the dog pits. At the same time, the last of the draped cages rumbled on, as though carrying its prisoner to the gallows. The armoured drayman jumped off the carriage and, aided by a couple of the Scarlet Circus dwarfs, he pulled away the Union Jack. The poor beasts gathered about the pit ready to fight were mute. The crowd also went silent, their mouths open with awe. By this time, the Fell Boy had crossed the cobbles and pushed his way through the mob to see what was in the final cage.

The beast was backed into one corner of the cage. Its colouring could not be seen, while it was shaped like a kangaroo endowed with the head of a pit-bull terrier. In the hush, the animal rose and stood on all fours. It moved close to the bars of the cage, and with its big black snout sniffed the air. There were murmurs from the crowd. Suddenly Captain Potter struck the bars with his sword and, like the crack of a whip, the beast lashed out at the side of the cage. This alarmed the mob, not just the noise of the Captain's sword striking the iron bars, but also the reaction of the beast. Fully exposed now, its colours could be seen. It was striped like a tiger, the thick streaks running half way up its back from its hind quarters. The muscles beneath its hide were hawsers, and its tail a lashing cable. It turned with shocking speed, and then all at once it opened its mouth in a giant yawn, so wide that the back of its throat could be seen, framed by jags of teeth.

Satisfied by the naked wrath of his beast, Captain Potter shouted at the top of his voice, "Is this not what you wanted to see? Have I not brought you something from the fiery depths!"

"Sir, I will wager one hundred guineas on this beast against any pit dog!" Tom Cribb cried, seeing the mettle of the devil dog. There was a resounding cheer from the crowd and all the pit dogs began to bark and howl.

"Well, thankee, Tom," the Captain said, "Now stand aside, ladies and gentlemen, while we bring the beast to the pit!" The whole manoeuvre had been planned. The dwarfs began to tumble along the ground, weaving in and out of the crowd. Their cavorting and mock fighting kept the crowd entertained, while the beast was taken from its prison through a wooden pen and into the pits. As it emerged into the steep-sided panelled arena, there were boos and cries of derision from the watchers. There were one or two ladies in the audience, including the old dowager Lady Matilda Dagobert, who stabled the majority of the fighting dogs gathered for the day. The handlers were there with their prickly sideboards, as grim and stern as the challengers in their charge. The first of these was the fearsome cross between a bull mastiff and a pitbull terrier. It had tremendous weight and a jaw strength that would crack bones and rip flesh.

The Fell Boy had managed to wriggle among the betting and the fury, the smell of greed and the stink of grown men gambling on dumb innocent animal blood. The beast stood proud, for it was intuitive from the wild. Rather than making for its adversary, it moved and sided against a board and presented itself as a target from only one angle. Then suddenly it shook itself, as it picked up the scent of the fighting dog set against it. Then it began to lope round the wooden slats of the circular pit, leaping and bounding with a free grace, more like a big cat than a canine combatant.

The tiger wolf dropped by the cage, where the crossbred mastiff was still held, to sniff the panting of its foe. Strangely, the dog stopped its baying and moved away from the bars, as if it was uncertain. Then the beast was off again. Now it appeared awkward and ungainly, as it shuffled carefully around the arena, savouring the stench and the sand where the previous canine combatants had been. The Fell Boy sensed what it might be thinking, 'Kill or be killed.'

The hold where the mastiff waited was opened by a group of men hauling on ropes, pulling up the cage front like a trap door. The mastiff bolted forth like a bull, confused and not knowing what lay in wait. As soon as it set eyes on the beast, it hunkered low. It had to strike out at the throat, grip hold of it and choke it to death or sever the jugular vein. The weights of the animals were more or less even, although the beast was not in the same condition as its adversary, on account of its confinement during the long sea voyage.

The crowd roared with blood lust, while the Fell Boy felt for the beast, as he did for all creatures persecuted by man. The mob was baying for the mongrel mastiff, while Lady Dagobert banged her silver-topped cane on the floor. "My God!" she cried to her mastiff as she saw it waver. "Show heart, my brave Trojan!" Even Captain Potter, who had some experience of the nature of the beast, stood back, holding his breath. The tiger wolf stood with its back to the wall, turning its head from side to side, checking the mastiff as it tried to butt in from different angles. The fighting dog was reluctant to take hold of the beast, as if it knew that it was being out manouvered. Time and again, it moved in close, and the beast adopted a cowering posture, lowering itself onto its muscular haunches, ready to get underneath the fighting dog's belly. The spectators were urging the mastiff to take hold of the beast about its neck, and Lady Dagobert's handlers were encouraging their dog from above. If they had dared to admit it, they were fearful. They had not seen this peculiar tactic in any other animal.

At last, the fighting dog came in close, but the beast seized its opportunity with diabolical timing. Its great jaws opened wide as an alligator. In one sharp movement, it clamped its teeth over the top of its enemy's skull, tearing a chunk of the bone clean off, so that the raw brain was showing. The bite was like taking the top off an egg. The fighting dog twitched once and uttered an unearthly howl, as it collapsed onto the sand. The beast jumped nimbly over the dog, and showed no further interest in the bloody mess darkening the sand. The clamour of the crowd became a sudden silence. All that could be heard was the panting of the beast. And the Fell Boy uttered under his breath, "Oh, Faerie King, King of the cross, thankee for saving the brave."

In her rage, Lady Dagobert was the first to break the hush. She stood up and pointed her silver-topped cane at Captain Potter. "This is no dog!" she screamed. "This beast has an unfair advantage. Will you wager ten thousand guineas against my best dogs, sir!"

Potter replied over the silence of the crowd, "I want your whole stock of slaves and the challenge is accepted, my lady."

By now, the beast had begun to lick at the blood of the mastiff with a delicate snake-like flick of its tongue, while the mob hissed in the background. Captain Potter's armoured handlers marched into the ring and dragged away the mastiff, one of them raking the sand to disperse the lost blood. And still the crowd hissed. The beast looked at the handlers distrustfully, yet showed no fear. Its long tiger tail switched from side to side, balancing the movement of its long head, which lolled up and down. Potter's gaze focussed once again on the Fell Boy, and he smiled as though he had found a lucky talisman.

Cribb held one of his arms aloft to get the attention of the Captain. He had taken to drinking a heavy dose of liquor, as soon as he had finished the trouble with the Irishman, so that he did not feel much pain. He saw Lady Dagobert making her way to see her other prized mastiffs and to meet her dog handlers outside the pens.

"Put the spikes on them!" she ordered.

"But, m'lady," the head handler murmured, "'tis not legal."

"Just do as I say, put the battle collars on. And as soon as you see my signal, release them immediately upon the beast."

Lady Dagobert's order shocked the handlers. Reluctantly, they began to fasten the spiked collars on to the two mastiffs. Already the smooth flanks of the mastiffs were damp with chilled sweat, as they were pushed into the wooden release pen to the words, "C'mon. C'mon, me boys. C'mon, lads" and, "You know what to do, my brave troopers." And indeed, the twin mastiffs had heads as large as the skulls of bears, their father a pit legend for having fought lions and hyenas.

A strange chanting was now heard around the dog pit, and the African hunters listened as if in a trance. The singing came from the cellars of Lady Dagobert's mansion nearby, where her slaves were penned. The Fell Boy was joyous, because he imagined that the far music was releasing him from the shores of England. And as the free Ethiopians heard the slaves, they too began to sing. The low deep human monotones made the tiger wolf look from the dog pit for its source, just as Lady Dagobert ordered her handlers to let loose the mastiffs. They bolted through the open cage door to meet the beast. Their red tongues slavered a fine viscous spittle down their sides, as they thundered from their enclosure. The cheering of the crowd now overlaid the jubilant singing of the African hunters. All eyes were now fixed on the middle of the pit.

The tiger wolf had sunk into a submissive posture, its tail low on the floor, brushing the sand between its legs. It trembled on its haunches and cowered, as though it was in fear. Now it scented more dogs, more pain, more punishment. Then there was a shout. "It looks like it is all over – 'tis turned yella!"

But the Fell Boy piped up, "Is not, is not, 'tis just pretending. Pretending to be scared."

The beast drew the mastiffs close. With courage, the lead dog, Hector, tensed his neck muscles, as he opened his powerful jaws, about to lock them onto the beast's neck and throat. Only the Fell Boy was wily enough to see the guile in the tiger wolf's eyes, the whites widening to flash a look of insolence and venom. At the same time, the beast squatted on its sturdy back haunches and tail, bearing its whole weight. From this low centre of gravity, it could use all its strength to lunge at the heavier mastiff. Hector hurled himself at the stink of his opponent. The mob was hushed at the prospect of a kill.

There was something very English about the combat, as the crowd willed a victory to the mastiff. But the tiger wolf was an unknown that nobody had ever seen, and it threatened the natural order of things. A primeval spirit was at work that had no rules to bind it. As the mastiff lunged, the beast opened its huge jaws and clamped them shut on the dog's nose at the front of its skull. The power and strength of the dog drained through its muscles onto the sand. Tightening its grip with its scissor teeth, the beast twisted with all its might, wrenching the lead dog onto its side. The mastiff's skull was crushed in one manoeuvre, but it was not dead. As the tiger wolf released its grip, the wounded fighter dragged itself away through the sand, dripping blood from its broken and ripped face.

Disgust wrenched the faces of the crowd. Some of them fingered their pistols, others looked away, while women fainted. Yet the horror was not over. The second mastiff, Spartacus, had leapt upon the tiger wolf's back. The grimaces and groans of the mob turned to cheering and howling, as the second dog pulled at the tiger wolf, trying to expose its soft underbelly for a killer grip. Lady Dagobert exulted, as though Spartacus could understand her. "Brave Spartacus! If you win, you shall enjoy a life of luxury and stud!"

Now the tiger wolf was beneath Spartacus, thrusting a huge head into its body, looking for flesh to tear. The powerful back legs of the beast enabled it to act as a big cat, with back swipes. Its powerful claws ripped Spartacus around its mouth. The dog now jumped off the beast and smelt its own blood escaping from the wounds. Spartacus snorted and snarled, as the tiger wolf flipped onto its right side and then to its feet, balancing perfectly with its long tail. The beast gave a low moan and moved towards the wooden boards of the circular pit, sliding round the outside of the arena again, dragging its short fur against the rough oak planks and growling without end. Spartacus manoeuvred quickly for another charge, determined to use its weighty body as a battering ram. Odds were now being offered in the crowd on Lady Dagobert's champion against the outsider, with its confusing and strange behaviour.

The Fell Boy hullooed as loud as he could from his vantage point. All through the chuntering and grimacing of the crowd, his tiny "Huzza, huzza!" could be heard, as though heralding some great change of fate for the tiger wolf. Apart from Captain Potter, who was in it for the money, the Fell Boy and the African hunters were the brute's only support.

Spartacus spun round quickly and stretched out its huge body, bounding across the pit and kicking up divots of sand and earth behind him. The tiger wolf froze. The crowd was triumphant, seeing a win for the bold Spartacus. The beast began to open its huge jaws in a macabre grin, trying to force itself against the wooden boards of the pit. But all the time, it was gauging the mastiff's speed and intent, and still it waited. Spartacus was doing what its ancestors had done against dogs and men for centuries. Its breed was the ultimate war dog. The great mastiff thrust on, but then, as if it had all been a lure, the wily tiger wolf reared up like a kangaroo, steadying itself on its strong back legs and tail, in the pose of a heraldic griffon without a shield.

It was enough. Spartacus missed its target and thundered into the barrel planking with tremendous force. There was a sicken thud, the fall enough to have slain a horse. The tiger wolf walked backwards on its hind legs, like a heraldic circus animal. It rolled its eyes as it went, and its ears twitched slightly on the top of its head, sensing another danger.

A spectator threw a walking stick at the tiger wolf in disgust, but it fell short of the creature's hind quarters. Others spat down, and one foolhardy man tried to slash at the beast with a sword, but was knocked out by one of the Captain's men. The mastiff rose groggily on its paws. Hardly knowing where it was, it went with tremendous fury at the pit boards on the opposite side. The tiger wolf bared its teeth, raising its black lips like theatre curtains. It sidled over to where Spartacus had crashed into the boards senseless. The ferocity of its charge had left it pinned to the slats by the combat spikes that Lady Dagobert had ordered. The mastiff's huge head lolled in the collar nailed to the wood. The tiger wolf jumped onto the back of the defenceless mastiff, clinging on with its powerful claws. Several ferocious bites later, the crowd was shouting obscenities at Captain Potter, who stood next to the militia guards holding the purse. The bite that finished the second mastiff came from the floor, as the tiger wolf locked its huge scissor jaws on to the top of its skull and took it off. Squirting blood, the mastiff's neck slid through the iron collar and its body lay twitching in its death throes at the feet of its foe.

The beast had silenced the crowd. Those ladies who could bear to watch fanned their faces and the men looked sidelong at each other. Two black streaks ran down the white powdered cheeks of Lady Dagobert, her angry tears taking the kohl from her eyes. The beast now paced round the perimeter of the dog pit, and looked up to where high in the sky, a buzzard was circling on watch. Surrounded by the African hunters in their full tribal costume, Captain Potter was protected from the anger of the mob and the fury of Lady Dagobert.

"I believe I now hold the purse," the Captain said, taking hold of a plump leather saddlebag, which held a fortune in coins of the realm. He struggled under its weight. One of the militia men, who had guarded the stakes, then shouted, "End the bloodshed this day! Please disperse! Time to see the circus!"

The Fell Boy could not help himself. He cheered at the top of his voice, and held his hands up in the air as though he was the victor. He cried out, "I want me Faerie King back! Gi' me back me Faerie King!"

Flanked by her burly dog handlers and private guards, Lady Dagobert approached Captain Potter. "Sir," she said, "take your hands off that money.

You assume that through this fraud you have become the authority in this town. You shall NOT take that stake and you shall NOT take my slaves."

"My lady," Potter looked into the air, "I am afraid your wager has already been taken and shall be divided among those gamblers who backed my beast." Lady Dagobert's guards drew their swords. "Lady Dagobert, you are well known for welshing on wagers. But not this time."

Although the militia had been paid off by Potter, they seemed to waver in their loyalty. But the African hunters drew their long spears and stood in a black wall in front of him. Their weapons spiked the air. Potter continued, "If you do not leave immediately, Lady Dagobert, we will have a man fight for five thousand guineas more. I have the vision. African hunters slay ice queen with her bully boys. I proclaim the crowd would want to see that."

Lady Dagobert looked at Potter's bodyguard, and ordered her men to put away their side arms. "Captain Potter, you are a villain and a traitor," she spat, "I shall see you hang." She spun round and bustled away, followed by her gang of guards.

Madness and mayhem erupted in Market Square. Bottles flew into the air and crashed down. Glass splintered over the cobbled streets. Figures fell drunk on the cobbles. Aldermen cavorted with the town harlots in front of their wives, who danced off with young rakes and scoundrels grown bold on Whitehaven rum. Order was running wild. Here and there drunks were stripping off, letting knives with iron blades cut stripes into their bare flesh. They were the beasts now. These were their blood games.

Captain Potter again jumped onto his wooden box, where he declared, "I give you the Fall of the Roman Empire! Another fantastic event from my menagerie and the Scarlet Circus!" He looked over to where the armoured handlers were gathered together. "Men, ye know what to do. Put the beast back in its cage and take it back to the ship! I want it well fed, and give it plenty water!" The noise from the Scarlet Circus troupe was now louder than the din of the crowd. Some of the dwarfs played exotic instruments from the East, while others sang a strange ungodly melody, as they paraded about the open square.

The rest of the menagerie exhibits were ready to be unveiled. The Giant Renaldo began his act by lifting an enormous barrel of rum above his head and pretending that he was going to dash it to the ground. This was met with cries of "Save the rum! Save the rum!" So instead, he set the barrel down gently on the cobbles. Then, with one blow of his fist, he smashed the top of the barrel in a spray of splinters. Cheering people ran forward, thrusting their heads into the barrel as if dunking for apples. Meanwhile, the dwarfs were muscling in and out of the mob, performing all sorts of lewd tricks.

Fire-eaters milled about, dressed as turbaned Indian princes and breathing flames from fire sticks. The war veterans were hacking away in mock sword-play. Staggering revellers were fainting and vomiting, and even the Fell Boy was frightened and shocked at the orgy.

In the middle of the square, a black spider monkey, dressed in the costume of a Dervish, scampered up a pole, chattering and screaming. It threw goose eggs on the townsfolk and the ducking and dodging street urchins. And now the dwarfs were leading the baboon-faced lady and putting her on show. Petch was booming at the top of his voice, "She is hairy all over! Give us a penny, and we will cut off a lock for your wig! It will chase the lice away. Cross me throat and hope to die!"

There was laughter from the men and haughty talk from the women. "My God, how vile!" And yet again, from another lady, "Monster, how you do shame us." Yet they still went past Petch and dropped their pennies into his bowl, peering at the baboon-faced lady's thatch of a face.

Still drunk from the evening before, ships' officers staggered from one spectacle to the other, brandishing their side-arms and yelling, "This one's for you, Boney! Ye'll face some British mettle!" Their boots shattered the empty rum bottles lying scattered on the streets. They raised their muskets with loud huzzas, toasting King George, who was too mad and far gone to hear them.

Captain Potter was hot with glory, and thinking about the prospects of what he could achieve with the winnings from the fight. He looked over to the armoured handlers, who had finished erecting the passage of slats into the beast's empty cage. It needed no encouragement to move back to where its own scent had been. It bounded back, looking about it as it went. Lady Dagobert's dead mastiffs were dragged out of the death pit, and their bodies flung onto one of her baggage wagons. The Captain's train of thought was broken by an uncanny feeling, as though the fingers of a ghost were being trailed through his hair. He turned to see the lightly powdered face of Meg holding her perfumed handkerchief to her nose. She looked at him with despair. "Have you not had enough money? Sir, your greed repels me! I can take no more of this. Don't you know that you have put yourself in so much danger that it will stop you ever coming back here again?"

Now the Fell Boy moved to where Potter was standing on his box, and tugged at his shirt cuffs. "I want me Faerie King back! I want me Faerie King back! And I want me passage on yer ship, away from this wicked place like ye said."

Potter's gaze moved from his sweetheart down to the Fell Boy. The effects of the laudanum and alcohol were wearing thin. Everything around

47

him was now a vexation to his soul. "Aye, boy, take your crosses. They're yours now and ye shall have a passage on my vessel. Ye shall sail as deck boy on the *Great Michael* with me, and I shall show you sights the likes of which no boy has ever seen before."

Meg tugged at Potter's arm, "Come, my dear, come and get some rest." Potter looked round and climbed off the box. Meg linked her arm through his, as if offering to shoulder some of his burden.

"My dear," he said, "I can give you anything you wish now."

She looked up into his eyes and said softly, "There is only one thing I want from you. Propose marriage to me before this sad day is out finished. Make it a happy day."

"Then we must go somewhere that is fitting for the occasion," Potter replied. "I shall take you to the secret caves. There there is a tiny chapel devoted to the Faerie King, as our little friend would have it. We can have some peace for a moment, contemplating the agonies of our Saviour, before I take your hand in marriage for all eternity."

Meg gently pushed a vial of laudanum into Potter's hand. He popped it into his mouth, opened his brandy flask and washed it down, grimacing and tightening his stomach muscles as the drug took hold. Then he turned again to the Fell Boy. "Explain to the Faerie King, my boy, how on September the seventeenth in the year of our Lord eighteen hundred and ten, Captain Potter of the seaport of Whitehaven became Prince of the World."

Now the captain was craning his head to search for men of his ship's colours. The Africans stood loosely in a pack around the final three cages of the menagerie train. Some of them had been watching the beast, and others were waiting for the order to rip the flags from the cages. Potter finally settled his gaze on Mr Bibington's outdated old-fashioned tricorn hat. By his side were several of the crew, including the bosun.

"Bibington! Now's yer chance to take command! I want ye to show the last exhibits, let loose the Scarlet Circus and I shall be back in an hour." He held Meg tightly round the waist with his right hand, squeezing it as he completed the order. "At long last," he continued, "I am to be married at the caves. Sssh, it's a secret!" He spoke so loudly that the sailors could hear him. Bibington was taken aback. "Aye, aye, Cap'n," he replied, and then he ordered, "Let's have beasties the animals on show! Let people see what we brought!"

As Potter and Meg slipped away, the flags were torn off the cages by the African hunters. The first of them was unveiled to reveal a huge lion. The drape of the Union Jack was now held at four corners by four of the merchant seamen. Bibington announced, "Look upon this ferocious lion and mind that this is symbol of our kingdom and if any man here dispute this fact, that we from the *Great Michael* are patriots here to entertain our nation, let him answer to us all."

The beast lion roared like artillery and shook its maned head, as if beset by bees or flies. The crowd shouted and threw money at the cage, which fell as hard drops of rain, an agitation on the lion's furious spirit.

"God save the King!" cried Bibington, backed by a volley of musket-fire. Then the Scarlet Circus put on a tableaux from 'Britannia Rules the Waves'. The Painted Lady played Britannia, her skin covered with a long flowing satin gown of red, white and blue, and in her hand a trident and shield. Bibington leapt in the air and began to dance a hornpipe. The crowd and the Scarlet Circus, and even the Fell Boy, joined in. The nation was kicking its heels in Market Square.

7

When the trouble began, nobody saw it coming. The Fell Boy was the first to notice that something was wrong. After losing both the fight to Tom Cribb and the crosses to Captain Potter, O'Connor was mightily aggrieved. The last thing he had left was his pride. His partner, the smaller and quicker Long, was hiding in a barrel under the lion's cage. He had his orders. As 'Rule Britannia' reached its crescendo, Long crept out of the barrel, drew his pistol and shot the lock off the cage. It sprang into the air and fell to the ground. With a deft movement, Long opened the cage door. The lion struck forward and bounded free. The brave African hunters ran for their lives, dropping their shields and spears.

Long was now pointing his second pistol at the lock on the gorilla's cage. There was a great flash and a resounding bang, but Long missed his mark. Before he had a chance to escape, Hudson Israel had driven his cutlass into the Irishman's guts. Long fell to the ground, coughing bright red blood all over his green tunic. Israel looked down at him and said, "Well, me lad, mischief maketh a poor mistress."

In the distance, the African hunters were running towards the *Great Michael*. "I knew them hunters was afeared," he said. His blade was drenched in blood. He bent down and wiped it on the dead man's coat, before sliding and clicking his sword back into its scabbard. He reached into Long's bulging pocket and removed a bottle of rot gut. "Now let's have a drink to 'ye on yer way," he said, uncorking the bottle and taking a generous swig. He then whistled at the top of his voice. An answer came back from somewhere in the crowd. Soon Petch appeared and looked down at the dead Irishman. Israel drew the dwarf close to him and whispered, "Go get our Cap'n. Ye'll find him at the caves with his wife-to-be. Our fates depend upon it." Petch rolled his eyes and then nudged the still warm body of the Irishman with his small boot. "And one other thing," Israel said, "O'Connor's ran off. Down near the harbour. We will sort him. Why don't ye send down Renaldo to pummel him once and for all?"

Petch said, "T'will be done." Then he dipped back into the crowd, picking up three other dwarfs and Renaldo, who knew as soon as he saw Petch's face the danger they faced. The strongman now pushed his way through the frightened crowd, making a passage for the four little people who followed him. It was like Moses parting the Red Sea.

Those near the lion were screaming. But so many people were packed into Market Square, that those further back did not realise what was happening. When the push came from the front, with the crowd trying to get away from the open cage, the revellers in the middle were knocked to the ground. Some of those still standing began to push back and lash out with their fists.

The Fell Boy was watching from his perch on a wall. His soul was happy that the lion was free. Now the big cat cut a swathe through the crowd and was pouncing on a lady, who was rigid with fear. The lion bit into her neck and shoulder and dragged her as a rag doll. Hudson Israel drew his pistols. Two muzzles flashed and thundered, as the seaman fired into its hind quarters. Bibington was looking down at his trousers, which were now wet with his own water. His legs were shaking and his hands twitched, as he saw the tragedy unfold. He was responsible and he knew it.

The lion was raging from the pain of one of the musket balls in its flesh. It dropped the lady, who was nearly dead, and took after a group of drunken naval officers. The lion leapt and began tearing at the backside of one of the officers. The militia scattered, every man for himself. Several more pistol shots were fired at the lion, but not one ball struck home. Ladies picked up their skirts and bobbled like jellyfish, while their menfolk cowered and scuttled off. A brave but foolhardy bystander slashed at the lion with his sword, but the big cat swerved and got hold of the man's head with its huge jaws. In one tearing twist, it left the body of its victim slumped against some old iron railings. With the man's head still in its mouth, the creature padded away from the fury and fear of the crowd up the hill towards St James' Church. In this apocalypse, he was the Beast from the Book of Revelation.

AS Renaldo and the circus dwarfs struck towards Whitehaven Harbour, the dragoons from the East Side battery were clattering into the town. They were led by Major Burkett, who had been warned of the riot by one of Lady Dagobert's handlers. Drunk on absinthe, she had commanded him to dash and warn the barracks. "Tell my nephew that Whitehaven is in danger of becoming completely lawless. He must send a contingent of dragoons with the greatest expedience. And take my best horse, Busephelis."

The hooves of the cavalry steeds struck the cobbles with authority and order, as they cantered into the town and descended through the streets towards Market Square. Major Burkett drew his sabre and ordered his unit to charge. The Cumberland troops were uneasy about the command from the start. One of the dragoons said under his breath, "Saints protect us! What in God's name is happening?" Another further along the line replied, "I seen one of them lions. Running like a banshee towards the church, he was." Leather creaked against polished brass and iron, as the dragoons reined back their powerful mounts. Froth began to appear at the sides of the mouths of the horses, and their flanks were wet and gleaming in the last light of the sun.

Major Burkett heard his men's small talk and exclaimed, "Steady, lads, we have a mission here today! We must show our teeth to get this rabble in order." He gripped his steed tight with his knees. He had never seen bloody action, as he was young, and he was eager to give a good account of himself. He shouted, "Sergeant Major! We have been ordered to round up the Scarlet Circus and take them to the local gaol. And nail a writ to the mast of the *Great Michael,* so that she cannot leave the harbour. We have the full cooperation of the Customs and Excise. Take fifteen men to the other side of Market Square. Position your dragoons there and wait. I'll signal by raising my sword. We surround them - any resistance, cut them down."

Through his spyglass, Captain Potter was watching the manoeuvres of the dragoons. He had already been married to Meg by a press ganged parson in the chapel in the caves. Now he and his new wife were blinking in the bright light, while Petch and three other dwarfs from the Scarlet Circus told them of the mayhem in the town. "Sir," Petch panted, "the lion's escaped. Several men dead. Dragoons on their way now. Connor did it. He ran away down the dock."

Potter looked at Meg. "We've had our break for the day and for the rest of our lives, my dear," he said. Meg looked down at her ring and then took it off, dropping it into her bosom. She drew out her small pistol. "As your wife, we'll both go down fighting then. To Heaven or Hades."

Potter stepped into action, "Aye, Petch, I have just seen the dragoons enter the town." He closed up his small spyglass. "We must tend to our own. Gather the cages together with the guards. I want you to cross country for the port of Harrington. We shall meet ye first light. They will not think to look there. If there is any trouble, take the animals into the wild and release them. We have made a king's fortune on this venture and we may yet have some more sport. We shall come for you."

In Whitehaven, the dragoons had begun to attack the Scarlet Circus and the menagerie. One of the dwarfs was ridden down by a dragoon. The townsfolk were scuttling for cover. Fine ladies threw off their shawls and hitched up their skirts and scarpered, followed by their intoxicated gout-ridden husbands. The faces of the crowd were contorted in terror, but the dragoons carried on, officers slashing at men who carried swords, or using the flat of the blade to lash at those who were stuck where they were.

The seamen from the *Great Michael* were holding back, until Captain

Potter appeared with Renaldo. The dragoons had seen Potter and were ordered to take him alive. Lady Dagobert was demanding her money back. The sailors formed a circle and waited for the dragoons to attack. Potter drew his side-arm, a grim Persian scimitar.

The Sergeant Major pointed his sabre at Captain Potter, screaming "Charge!" Before the horse had got within ten yards of him, Renaldo had picked up another rum barrel and hurled it, smashing the horse's limbs into kindling and downing the Sergeant Major. Now Potter slashed at the downed dragoon's throat, killing him with the stroke. This was the guarantee that he would hang. He drew his pistol and ended the horse's misery by shooting it through the head. Inspired, the sailors began to fire their pistols at the dragoons, and several more fell from their saddles. The Scarlet Circus now joined the fray, for they too had nothing to lose. They were used to the cut and thrust of battle and dispatched more of the dragoons. Potter moved with his circus squad to where the seamen were. "Lads!" he shouted. "Make for the *Great Michael*! Ready to sail as soon as ye can! We shall force our way through!"

In all, there were ten downed dragoons, seven of whom were dead. The wounded horses were stampeding away from the action. Captain Potter had lost two of his seamen, including his bosun, who had been shot through the heart. Another of the caged animals had been killed, a snow leopard, its white coat stained red with its blood. The huge cages were made ready to be moved. Everybody worked like the devil, knowing that this was their last venture on England's shores. Ahead lay the high seas or a noose. Behind them, Market Square was a slaughterhouse. Blood ran in the gutters, while the corpses of men, women and animals lay at random. Drunks lay next to the dead, so they could barely be told apart. And the windows were being boarded, the doors locked, in the brick tombs of the rich.

WHEN Lady Dagobert arrived with her coach and horses outside St James' Church, she was quite put out. The lion had been lying on the steps of the church, chewing the head of its victim. The musket ball had holed the big cat, and the open wound was dry with congealed blood. The lion gnawed the head like a kitten playing with a ball of wool. When it saw the coach horses, it viewed them as it would an antelope or a buffalo. Roaring loud, it leapt over the church railings on to the back of one of the screaming horses. The coachman jumped off the coach and ran for his life. The horses bolted, the team careering down the hill towards Market Square. The lion clawed into the lead horse and twisted into the throat of its prey.

Lady Dagobert barked at the coachman who had jumped. "My God, what are you doing? Where are we going?" She craned her wigged head out of the coach window to see the awesome spectacle of her horses being driven by a lion. Presented with this nightmare, she pulled her head in and fainted on the coach floor. Outside, the lion dragged down the first horse in the team, making the other horses teeter over on top of it. One of the metal-rimmed wheels broke from its axle with a crack, tipping the coach on its side. The coach door opened and Lady Dagobert was thrown prostrate onto the cobbles.

Captain Potter and some of his men had seen the runaway coach, but they had to hoist sail. The Scarlet Circus were also making their way to the *Great Michael* with their gear and props, though two of the dwarfs and Renaldo stayed with the cages to support the armoured guards. Major Hackett and the surviving dragoons had gone to muster as many of the local militia as they could, as well as any good citizen who would fight. Potter knew of this. He was spurred on to set sail in the *Great Michael*. He shouted out to Petch, "Take this money. Ye may need it. Three thousand guineas – take yer share and divide the rest. What is left, ye can return on the ship."

Petch nodded, "Aye aye, Captain." He then cried out to the cage handlers and the Scarlet Circus. "Get on! We must make Harrington before the soldiers come back."

Potter was morose, "If ye have to, Petch, release the animals. Give them a fighting chance." He turned on his heel and, taking Meg's arm, made for the ship. The Fell Boy ran after them and tugged at Potter's silver cuffs. He would stay with the cages. "I'll help the circus train, Cap'n. Best for me to be with Coocoolin. I'll go with them. I'm with Coocoolin."

Meg took pity on the boy and stroked his head. "Don't fret, we are all done for now. You come with us on the *Great Michael*. Follow the cages to Harrington. We shall meet you there."

So the menagerie set off slowly on the old smugglers route. As they moved away, Captain Potter looked at the tiger wolf and saluted. "For God's sake," he cried after the train, "look after the champion!"

The Fell Boy ran up to Petch at the head of the horses pulling the cages. "I must fetch me fox, Petch." And the dwarf answered, "No need, boy. He got out of the Red Admiral. Go on, bark for him. He knows your call."

So the Fell Boy threw back his head and coughed and howled. And the red fox came running to them over the bodies of the dead. His paws passed over the corpse of Mr Bibington, whose stiff white hand pointed the way that the Scarlet Circus and the menagerie were taking. Captain Potter's luck had run out. As he and Meg reached the *Great Michael*, he found two armed Customs men waiting for him.

"Looks like ye're done, Potter," one of them said.

The Captain replied like ice, "I think ye're pushing yer luck, sir." He went to draw his concealed pistol, but then he saw two of his crew covering the Customs officials with their weapons.

"Now, Mister Potter, if ye were to drop that plump bag of guineas, I'm sure we could turn a blind eye like Admiral Nelson on yer sail away."

"Sir, you dishonour me," Potter said. "Have I not already given you one thousand guineas today?"

"So you have, sir. But ye got not much choice in the matter. I think we should have those guineas."

One of the sailors on deck pointed his pistol at the excise man and pulled the trigger. There was a flash and a lead ball hit the blackmailer on his shoulder, sending him tumbling on the dockside.

"Get out of my way, sir, before you receive the same," Potter hissed. "We go where no man shall follow and no man can find us." He and Meg jumped onto the gangway and made for the foc'sle. "Cast off! Set the top sails! We must draw away!" And in two shakes, the vessel began to move towards the dock gates. "Well done, lads, but we're not finished yet. Man the cannons. Look lively. We'll share out the loot. You are all due a piece. I said you would receive more guineas on one trip with me than if you served in the Royal Navy for twenty years. We must get out of these waters."

BACK on land, the twitching parson of St James was opening the church doors onto the graveyard. He met the sight of a huge lion yawning on top of a dead horse, and contemplating which part of his prey to start on first. Lying next to the twisted frame of the coach, like a discarded marionette, was a senseless woman. Her billowing skirt could not hide the frailty of her aged body. Her wig lay next to her face, exposing shaven white hair that hugged the contours of her small head. Her red ball shoes, buckled in silver, pointed out as if her ankles were broken. The figure stirred and leaned forward on its rump end. Lady Dagobert now began to take in her situation, and was trembling at the prospect of meeting her maker. What would the demon of a lion do to her? She had witnessed the dogs ripping each other apart in the pits. Now the lion was greedily feasting on the tender neck of the horse. She began to crawl across the cobbles. Would she still save herself and have her revenge on Captain Potter? Even the parson was wondering if he should aid this foul old matriarch.

The lion gnawed on, roaring from time to time, as if to warn away vultures and scavengers, like the crawling woman. The parson was shuffling at the church door, trying to get her attention without drawing that of the lion.

She could see him quite clearly, but she was also trying not to enrage the lion, which seemed to know that they were near. As it gorged the succulent horseflesh, it spied Lady Dagobert crawling away. The parson looked up at the Almighty and prayed half-heartedly for the safety of the old lady. As if in answer to his prayer, the lion turned its nose up at the aged morsel and contented itself gnawing its fresh meal.

Cumberland began to wake up from the nightmare. The shutters on the mansion doors were flung open by servants. The menfolk appeared on the steps of their houses with blunderbusses, shotguns, pistols and muskets. They had wakened from their fright and were now ready to take control again. Moreover, the militia had mustered. Troops of them marched through the streets and alleys towards the town centre.

The *Great Michael* was lurching through the harbour gates on light sails, her crew bearing arms on port and starboard, with her cannons made ready. Potter and his new bride stood at the wheel, possibly on their last stand. Lights flickered on in the harbour watch towers, where the militia had taken control. The balance of power was changing, as the swift merchantman made for the open sea. Then the Captain called out, "Fire a broadside at the towers, me dandies! Let them know who we are!" A barrage of cannon balls exploded into the stone forts by the docks.

Major Burkett gave the order to fire from the shore battery. The guns responded, loosing their shot from their nine-pounders at the *Great Michael,* which was sliding out of range. Balls fell into the sea short of their target, spraying plumes of water high into the air as they seared the waves. The *Great Michael* was pushed along by following winds, out of the range of the battery. Captain Potter ordered, "Break out the rum! The last time any man took the port of Whitehaven, it was a damn Yankee. Here's a toast to John Paul Jones! We steer north east for Harrington. And then on to Australasia! Any man who wants to go ashore in the longboat, now is his chance. We shall never set eyes on old Albion again."

The Captain waited for some response from the crew, but there were no takers. All were bound now to the *Great Michael,* wherever she would end.

8

The fleeing circus train rolled and rumbled into the night, passing through the outskirts of Whitehaven. The animals seemed to know to be silent, for there was no sound, no bark, no scream, no howling. The Fell Boy stuck close to the circus dwarfs and held onto his fox's leash. Behind them the lights of Whitehaven became prickles in the dark, as they went down the old smugglers' track through Elfanghyill Valley.

The cage drivers and guards had taken off their heavy body armour. The moonlight glanced off their shiny faces and sweaty backs, as they moved their heads this way and that, on the look out for the militia and the Excise men. Petch strode the length of the carriages, encouraging the tired and beleaguered circus. The Painted Lady held on to the bars of one of the cages, carried along a foot off the ground in her great gown.

"All right, all right, me bravos," Petch said, "let's have a wee rest. I took the trouble to load a barrel of rum in the square, so let's have a farewell noggin to old England."

The cages drew to a halt and Petch took down the liquor barrel, striking it with a fid, so that the spirits flowed from the open barrel. One at a time, each circus member and guard took turns at drinking from the trickle of fire. Even the Fell Boy took a sip and was told to drink more by the dwarfs. "C'mon, boy, ye're not far from being a man. Take a bigger draught."

The scarred faces of the guards pushed close to the barrel, as they drank deep from it. Some coughed and spluttered, while others let the rum run down their shirts, so that they could sniff the spirits all night long.

Petch strode forward again. "Right, ye scallywags, let's be moving ahead." He drove a spigot into the hole made by the fid and stemmed the flow of rum from the barrel.

The cages creaked on down the secret track. The Fell Boy looked for signs of movement in the tiger wolf's cage, but it was curled up tightly in a mound. Every so often, it would lick its wounds and tuck its head under its paws to carry on sleeping. And more than anything, the Fell Boy wanted to stroke the beast. He moved round to the opposite side of the cage, where nobody could see him, and he put his hands through the bars onto the striped hair of the beast, patting its fur. There was no response, so the Fell Boy thought it must be asleep. But as he moved away, the beast briefly opened one eye.

As they entered a hard slate cutting on the path, dark shadows indicated caves in the rock face. In one of these stood a figure that could only have been Lanty Slea, the smuggler. Scanning the area for further signs of trouble, Petch could see Slea's men on their way up from the beach, bringing in loads of tobacco, rum and cognac. Petch knew that anyone on the track would be charged a high toll for passing through. From his hideout, Slea was weighing up the cages, before he spat a mouthful of tobacco juice at the circus caravan. Then, crouching down in the opening of the cave, he lit a small lantern, so that the rock flickered with a dull yellow glow.

The dwarfs and guards pulled up their horses. Petch muttered to one of the drivers, "I think you better halt here. We got company."

Slea moved to the brink of the cave and looked down at the menagerie. "Right, me beauties," he called out, "that's far enough on ol' Lanty Slea's track and ye aren't paid up." A bag of bones, he took up his little lantern and seemed to drift towards the circus. Petch knew of Slea's reputation, so the dwarf stepped forward to look him squarely in the eye. "Well, sir, how much for our safe passage to Harrington? Here, you see, circus folk. No soldiers, no Excise men."

Slea towered over Petch and said, "I heard talk of yer trouble in Whitehaven and yer captain gone off with his gold. I need some of that." Armed smugglers were now gathering like standing stones among the rocks, while the cage drivers drew their cutlasses. Slea took a step back and fingered his pistols, tucked down the side of his belt. "Lay them down," he said. "Or pay the consequences. Everybody pays one way or the other round here."

The tiger wolf stirred in its cage as did the panther. Sensing the menace around them, the beasts had come to life. Slea's men became uncertain. Petch seized the moment. As Slea had taken a step back, so the dwarf took a step forward. "Hokey pokey, sir," he said. "We got swords and pistols too. To give no quarter to get none." He pointed at the great beasts in their cages. "And if you want them on your backs too..." The tiger wolf gaped.

At that Slea stooped so that his face was level with the dwarf's. "Why, if titch isn't spoiling for a fight." His men moved into the middle of the path, as did the cage drivers and the dwarfs, to confront the others, with the Painted Lady and the Fell Boy close behind. Petch looked Slea in the eyes and said defiantly, "We are not spoiling for a fight, sir, but you are. Now what is it to be? Fight or deal." Petch heard the hammers on the pistols of the smugglers click back.

But Slea gave him a smile as thin as a cut-throat razor, saying, "Well, game chicken, the toll of the track is six hundred guineas. Then ye get safe passage to Harrington. Now those lads in red and blue, we don't like them.

So what goes to you come cheap." Slea signalled to his men to uncock their pistols. The cage drivers and guards stepped well back behind Petch, the fighter turned negotiator. "Better to barter," he said, "than back off. How about five hundred guineas for our safe passage to Harrington? And when we are there, one hundred guineas more. You are a man of honour, so they say."

"I is and I is not - Yes and no," Slea answered, "but if I had any respect for yer cap'n, ye would pass by free. Half pint ye maybe, but ye're twice the man he is. Deal done."

Petch nodded to one of the cage guards to bring the bag of guineas, which he counted, giving the purse to the smuggler. "Here is our part of the deal. Now we must be on our way."

"Ye're two mile from Whitehaven and another eight mile to Harrington. Fork up ahead, take left side and ye'll make it by cockrow, ye damn bantam. Ye can have two of my men for company, just to put ye on track."

So the caravan moved on, escorted by two armed smugglers, who walked in front. The younger one was surly and silent, but the older one knew a circus guard, the one with the sword slash across his blind eye. "Will," he said, "ye've been hurt bad and cut about face by Boney. I always knew ye as a vengeful man. Did ye settle them good?"

The guard peered through his good eye. "Nay, Jamie, I was not able to settle the account. I was cut down by three of Boney's guard at Carunna. They stuck me with their bayonets. No pension neither. When I come back home, it were only for the likes of Cap'n Potter that I was in work again. The Captain's different."

Winding along the shoreline, the small port of Harrington came in sight. Fishing schooners were tied up against the wharf, ready to strike out into the Irish Sea, their white sails like tents afloat in the dawn. Lights twinkled from riggers' and carpenters' workshops, late into the night. The sea was whipping up. Every now and again, the waves broke upon the rocks in foam that seemed all the whiter against the dark ink seas of the Solway Firth.

Petch ran towards the first of the cages and jumped up next to the driver. "Give me the eyeglass. Quick. That is the *Great Michael's* lights, I tell ye." There were murmurs of excitement and relief from the circus troupe and the guards, but the monkeys were huddled together in their cage, trembling at the night and the other beasts nearby. The Fell Boy could smell their fear. It brought back the stench of the men in Whitehaven. The two smugglers now stopped ahead of the circus train and, as the first of the cages drew level with them, the surly one said, "Where's one hundred guineas more for Lanty's chest, runt?"

"My name is Petch. Here is the rest of the gold." Petch tossed a leather bag down into the hands of the smuggler.

"Thankee, sir." This time, the young smuggler was humble. "We be leaving now. God speed to yez." Like spectres, the smugglers vanished into the night. And on the distant water, the *Great Michael's* lanterns shone brighter as she drew nearer to the fishing port. Her sails swelled above the choppy firth, while a Yankee flag fluttered from her stern.

The Fell Boy was not watching the sea, but staring at the tiger wolf, which was pacing round its cage, sniffing the sea breeze. It held its head low to the cage floor as if the weight of its head was too heavy for its neck, its striped tail twitching from side to side. The fox strained on its leash, trying to pull away from the cage. The beast was fixing on the cage door, where instead of a lock, somebody had fastened the catch with a knife. It stood on its hind legs like a man and shuffled towards the bars, balancing on its back paws and tail as it went. It looked down at the Fell Boy. He had to take out the knife. He shook his head to get rid of the grogginess of the rum. He looked up again and saw the beast looming above in menace. Its great back claws scraped on the wooden floorboards as it balanced against the cage door.

The Fell boy could take no more. He let loose the fox's leash and sidled round the back of the cage, taking hold of the bars. He could feel the warm breath of the beast on his cheek, as he gently removed the knife from the catch. Now the beast's claw grazed the palm of his hand. It stayed close to the boy all the time he was setting it free. In front of the circus train, Petch held up his hand. "We have one hour to load these animals onto the *Great Michael*! If it were me, I would let them go." As he spoke, the beast nudged open its prison door and leapt on to the track. Nobody but the Fell Boy saw it bound away into the breaking dawn.

THE *Great Michael* had made good headway in favourable winds, which took her through the stone breakwater of Harrington Harbour. There the vessel waited, tied to the wharf. The Cumberland and Westmorland militia were on their way, and a naval frigate from Dumfriesshire on patrol was looking for the pirate vessel. The captain was in no mood for delay. The voyage from Whitehaven had been short and the safety of his ship was his first duty. Now he had to see to the circus and the menagerie, and so he set off to find them. And when he did, he began to shout at Petch. "For God's sake, Petch, we will have to shoot these animals! We have no time, we must get rid of them now!"

"Even the beast, sir?"

The Fell Boy could hold his tongue no more. "He's gone. Coocoolin's gone. He stood up on his hind legs like a man and opened the door and beat it."

The Captain looked at the Fell Boy and shook his head, grinning. "My God, boy, you have seen some sights. I wager one of these buffoons gave you too much grog." He darted over to the beast's cage and examined it, as if he thought the creature might somehow be hiding beneath a trap door. "Petch! Let the others go!" he ordered. "Open the doors and turn them loose!"

The cage doors were flung open. The monkeys, the panther, the two-headed goat, everything was released into the darkness. They all bolted.

"Now get yourselves aboard. You are tied body and soul to me for the rest of your days. We have a crew, we have provisions and we have a destination." His voice was now low with melancholy, "On to Van Diemen's Land!"

One after the other, the twenty strong circus troupe, the Fell Boy and the fox ran up the gangway of the *Great Michael*, followed by the drivers and the guards. Captain Potter had remained true to his word, as had the smugglers and the Fell Boy. For he had promised that he would free the beast, and so he had done. As the *Great Michael* heaved away from the shores of Cumbria for the last time, the militia and the Excise men arrived in Harrington and were inspecting the empty cages. Captain Burkett looked out to where the ship was moving out towards the horizon. He held up his spyglass. Twisting it into focus, he could see a freak show jerking their hands up at him, as he shouted, "Send word to the Admiralty and the Harbour Commissioners of Whitehaven! We have lost the *Great Michael*. She is bound due west."

WHILE they were blaming each other for not reaching Harrington sooner, the Excise men were not aware that they were being watched. The beast looked down on them from a high crag. Behind it, sodden grey clouds scudded across the wispy sun. They shed light on the beast intermittently, but never long enough to show its size and nature. Cu'chulain raised his hammer head and scented the air. He had not eaten for near on a day and hunger gnawed inside his ribs.

Cu'chulain clambered down the rock face on to the springy turf stretching out before him. He had picked up the scent of a fat sheep, and so he loped off, using the cover of the hedgerows to protect himself from squinting eyes. The beast was back on the prowl. He had suffered the savagery of man, the sea and other animals. Now he was free to hunt and feed. He slunk downwind to a grazing flock of Herdwick ewes on his left flank, and he moved into the open field below them. There he squatted on his haunches and waited.

He was watching a plump and sweet-smelling ewe. Hungry as he was, Cu'chulain stayed low. The grass in which he lay was damp with dew. Ordinarily he might have rolled about like a playful pup, kicking his legs into the air joyful in the smells of the earth. His mouth slavered over his forelegs as his quick dark eyes gauged the ewe's position. Then he launched himself off his hind legs, as powerful as those of a lion, while his forelegs were those of a wolf. The ewe did not even have a chance to look up from the grass she was nibbling. Cu'chulain crushed the ewe's windpipe and severed its jugular vein in one lightning snap of his immense jaws. It took time for the rest of the flock to realise that another ewe had been killed by an intruder. Then all of a sudden, the flock shifted and scattered across the field away from the scene of death.

Cu'chulain gnawed for several minutes on the dead ewe, savouring the warm blood and tearing the skin, so that he could get at the succulent meat. During his feasting, he rose on all fours and looked about, using his eyes and scenting the air for danger. He then began to disembowel the animal, digging deep for the liver and kidneys. Once satiated, he moved on in search of other prey, his striped sides swollen with the pounds of meat and blood he had devoured. Instinct took him towards the rocks and shale. These were hard places for any pursuit, and he had to sleep where he could not be found. He wanted to digest his meal in peace. Apart from sheep, there were only small rodents and the odd bird trying to sleep between the cracks of the dry stone walls. There was no danger here, and so Cu'chulain set off for a large mound, where there were standing stones that would provide shelter and comfort. He saw the rocks as frozen mammoths guarding a place of dark repose, a bastion of solitude.

The dew on the grass clung to the fur on his legs and shimmered every time a ray of light beamed down from between the scuds of cloud. His great tongue flopped loosely down the side of his mouth, his lower jaw heavy and eyelids on the droop. As the standing stones came nearer, he stopped and sighted a hollow in the earth beneath one of the fallen stones. Inching further forward, he used all his senses to check for other occupants, a badger or some other rival. Then, knowing he was safe, Cu'chulain entered into the darkness and settled down on the warm earth. He licked his lips and face in an attempt to clean his fur of the sheep's blood, but he soon gave up. Curling up and placing his head tight between his front legs, he fell into a deep sleep, a pack heaven where he could dream about his own kind.

9

A poacher wandered into the field where the tiger wolf had killed the ewe. He came across the half-eaten carcass, and what he saw frightened him. This was not the kill of a stray dog or fox, for whatever creature had done this had drunk blood and eaten only certain parts of the carcass to satisfy its hunger. The poacher bent down and grabbed the ewe to see what was on the other side of it. The sheep turned over easily, as it was stiff as a board. He noticed that the animal's liver and kidneys had been removed through two gaping holes in its stomach. He dropped the dead ewe and looked about cautiously. "Tis work of devil," he muttered to himself, "or the work of a witch, even." He had an old sack with him that contained a snared hare and two rabbits. He threw this back over his shoulder and ran back to his village.

From his lair, Cu'chulain had smelt the poacher and, from a crouch, he watched the man cross the field and climb over a wall. The smell of the dead ewe lingered in his nostrils. He marked his territory before he left, pissing a thick jet of strong-smelling water over the base of one of the standing stones. He then moved off into the prevailing light wind, so that he could have advance warning of the presence of other men. He could cover fell after fell to track down his prey, while a distance of thirty miles was a mere outing. He made for the smell of fresh water drifting on the air. He would need to lap deep and long.

LAW and order were now being restored in Whitehaven in the customary manner. The Cumberland and Westmorland militia had regrouped, continuing their task of shooting or bayoneting anyone who could not get out of the way. Several people had been rounded up and bundled into cellars that had previously held slaves. These were to be the examples, their fate a public execution on the gallows.

The African hunters had run out of luck and were surrounded. Cold and hungry, they had not gone very far and were on the point of surrender. The militia's guns were trained on the Africans, who threw down their small spears and bull-hide shields. Suniman stepped forward. He bowed his head to Major Burkett in submission.

"Sergeant Major! Put them in chains and take them to Clifton Hall!" The militia jumped down from their horses and manacled the hunters, who growled as caught wild animals.

The prisoners were marched to Clifton Hall, Lady Dagobert's summer and autumn residence. Flanked by mounted militia, their chains rattled, hanging in loops between them. Every so often, a kind soul from a nearby cottage or farmstead would offer them food and drink. Knots of people gathered to watch the spectacle, for in these parts it was unusual to see slaves with their heads so high.

By late afternoon, the captives had reached the gatehouse at Clifton Hall, where they were met by overseers and estate men. News had reached there not long after their taking, and Lady Dagobert was already in the process of cutting any losses. Overcoming much pain from her leg wounds, she appeared on the front steps with her estates manager, Thomas Curwen.

"Consider these men returned to the purpose for which they were intended!" she ordered. "I have had reports of a slaver in the port of Lancaster due to sail next week. I want them all, including those in the cellars, marched to Lancaster to meet this ship without delay. You can take them across the sands of Morecambe Bay. This will cut down your marching time. We shall sell them on the block on her return to The Carolinas. Manacle them in the cellars with the rest. Five days from now, we shall embark on another profitable journey."

BY the time the shepherd found the dead ewe in the field the following morning, the tiger wolf was more than ten miles gone. For the shepherd, this was the most serious of crimes, a hanging matter. One of his flock had been murdered. His poor confused sheepdog cowered next to his master's boots. It could smell the scent of the tiger wolf and shivered with fear.

"Come now, Jack," the shepherd said, "you've seen this before." But why was the dog so shaken? "I must get word to Farmer Thornthwaite we have a wild one at large."

MATILDA, Lady Dagobert, was reclining in her drawing room. Her spindly legs were newly bandaged and rested on a satin pouffé, while her complexion was its usual ashen colour. She was startled by a loud knocking at the main entrance, which was promptly opened. She heard the words, "Please enter and follow me" and counted the footsteps.

The drawing-room doors creaked open, and her butler entered the room. He was a handsome black man, wearing a white wig and gloves and green britches. His dainty black shoes were ornamented with silver buckles. Traipsing behind the servant, clutching his cap and a small casket and keeping his eyes firmly on his feet, was a man who looked like he had not washed for some time. As they entered the drawing-room, the butler declared to

Lady Dagobert in impeccable English, "Mister Alfred Wheaton, ma'am. tradesman."

"Who?"

"Mister Alfred Wheaton, ma'am. Tanner and knacker, ma'am."

For a brief moment, Lady Dagobert's face lit up. "Aah, very good, Richmond. That will be all." As the doors closed, she snapped at Wheaton "Well, did you get them? Have you brought the teeth?"

"Yes, yer l-ladyship," he stammered. "As requested, me l-lady, here are the l-lion's teeth." Wheaton opened the casket and handed it to her.

She picked at the contents, the lion's fangs, and inspected them closely. "Aaah, these are superb, Wheaton. And tell me, how long will the taxidermist take to prepare the animal for presentation?"

"It won't be l-long now, me l-lady. He's got his best men working on it now. So, b-begging yer pardon, me l-lady, we would need the l-lion's teeth back."

Lady Dagobert glowered at Wheaton. "Yes, I know that. I only wanted to make sure the job had been done properly. Have you news of any of the monkeys?"

"Well, they managed to shoot two of the bigger ones and they are down at the barrack house. They need to be inspected by the doctor." Wheaton looked increasingly uncomfortable. He took his eyes from the floor and looked up at the high ceiling. "There was some talk of them being French spies, me l-lady."

Lady Dagobert sat back in her chair in mock astonishment. "What tricks will Boney stoop to next?" she exclaimed before dismissing Wheaton with a wave of the handkerchief she was holding to her nose. "Now, next time I see you, I expect the lion to be with you." She handed him back the teeth. The young butler stepped forward and ushered the man out of Clifton Hall. Lady Dagobert reached for her quill and paper, dipped the point into the ink pot and began to write to her friends and associates. The first letter was to her nephew, General Colonel William Birkett, at Carlisle Castle.

My dearest William,

Although I was spared from the savagery of that monstrous animal, I am suffering the most severe leg wounds. I know you will do everything in your power to catch and apprehend the evil instigator of Saturday's treacherous events. I am respectful of your attentions to date, and I thank you sincerely for alerting His Majesty's Navy since that vile pirate, Captain Potter (for that is what he is), was seen sailing out of the Solway Firth two days ago. As you know, I have some considerable influence in London and I intend to secure the services of a privateer, who shall be on the lookout also for that

abomination of a man.
I am, sir, your obedient and most humble servant.
Matilda
P.S. On your next visit to Clifton, you will see that I have had that raven-ous lion stuffed! The Cumberland and Westmorland militia deserve the greatest of respect for their services to the Crown.

THE wind had dropped and Ennerdale Water was calming, but Cu'chulain had had a fitful night's sleep. He had taken his time in his journey to the lake, for he had not picked up on the manky man smell since the poacher the day before. Sometimes he was so sensitive that he could see a light fog clinging to a gatepost or on top of a wall, and even a man's footprint, for the tiger wolf could see smell. He lived on meat, and the scent of mutton was sweet, but the smell of man was sour and stank of danger. Moving closer to another fine Herdwick ewe, Cu'chulain began to drool on the grass, as he pulled himself close to the ground to stalk his victim. When he was within leaping distance, he bounded into the air and fell on top of his prey, clawing it to the ground. Before the sheep had time to struggle, Cu'chulain killed it instantly by crushing its windpipe and severing its arteries in one twisted bite.

When the rest of the flock heard the ewe thud onto the heather, they skit-tered off along the lake shore. When they thought they were safe, they car-ried on eating as if nothing had happened. Cu'chulain gorged on the choic-est pieces of the ewe. He tore at the soft muscle-flesh still warm with blood around his victim's neck. He devoured several pounds of flesh and drank some of the ewe's blood. Before he left to find shelter and sleep off his meal, he opened up the sheep's stomach and teased out its liver. Then away he roamed to find some other hidden place, still holding the innards in his jaws.

THE alarm had been raised. The shepherd had sounded the alert. The hunters and hounds were put in a meet in the field. Off they all went, march-ing across the countryside dressed in their traditional Cumbrian hunting grey. Finally, here was their chance to kill something other than a fox or a hare. This was the big game.

10

THIS new hunt over the fields and fells soon drew the attentions of the local newspapers. Three days into the chase the Ennerdale pack had dispatched fourteen foxes, and one of the huntsmen had shot a hare with his pistol. One of the terriers was lost down a badger's sett and severely mauled by the time it was retrieved. But there was no sign of the beast, only much talk about the nature of the killer at large. Most of the huntsmen were agreed that they were in pursuit of a large dog.

"Well," one of them said, "I have heard that John Peel himself maintains 'tis a girt dog, but he also said it had the mark of a mad killer."

"Well, lad," replied another, "we be having nay luck. We canna get anywhere near this beast, so perhaps Mister Peel may be so kind as to give us a hand."

That same evening, as darkness drew down over the fells, the huntsmen did get near their quarry. Just as the dying sun began to cast a red orange shadow over Ennerdale Water, Cu'chulain emerged from his lair, his rusty stripes blending into the twilight. He picked out the shapes of the horses, men and hounds, searching on the flat banks of Ennerdale Lake. Upwind, he was safe. Suddenly the sound of the hunting horn blared up the valley. The wind turned and the terriers caught the scent of the beast. Thrown into a frenzy, the lead dogs bayed and snarled, and the lesser dogs of the pack whimpered with fear.

Cu'chulain was off - he made across the tops of the hills and where he could, he ran through water. Sometimes he took gulleys where streams gouged out dark hollows on their way into the lake. Up above the banks of a stream, more sheep grazed. Cu'chulain took his chance. He clambered up the steep bank, relying on his powerful back legs, and pulled a ewe into the stream to kill it. Gorged on meat and blood and water, Cu'chulain slunk down the bank into a dark pothole, where there was no life apart from a few bats clinging to the roof. In this stone womb and in the still comfort of the darkness, the angry spirit of the beast was given peace. In his heart he had willed armies of his own kind to pack behind him and hunt down the men in grey over the hills, so that he could turn the murder back on his persecutor. Yet he was now here alone. Confronted with the man spirit, he crawled further into the cavern away from their scent until he came to a place that was still and warm. He stretched out on a ledge along a damp face of slate rock and rested his head next to a dark pool of water. The drip of a hundred drops resounded on the dark viscous surface. The odour of damp moss obliterated any other scent. Straining his eyes to see what might appear around the crag, he scratched his underbelly with sharp hind claws and dropped his leg back on the ledge. Cu'chulain felt as a young pup, close to his mother's breast. A sigh escaped his mouth in a wisp of frosty vapour.

The stream was whipped into a lather, as the foxhounds of the Melbreak Hunt fell upon the scent of their quarry. The whippers-in, who were dressed in grey coats and carried muskets, whipped the pack on. The lead huntsman, Josiah Nape, knew the land well. He blew loud on his hunting horn. The baying and barking of the hounds would disturb the rest of the night.

"C'mon, lads, c'mon, lads!" he shouted to his dogs. "C'mon, let's have a look in this cave. There's something in there!" To his lead dog he shouted, "What ails ye? C'mon, Ned, lead away!" Ned bolted through the waters towards the pothole entrance. He seemed to get the scent, then lose it, then get it again. This confused the rest of the foxhounds thrashing in the stream.

Josiah Nape jumped off his gelding and into the water. Deep inside the recess, Cu'chulain rose onto his hind feet and stood motionless, taking in the scents of the intruders through twitching nostrils. "I will have this beast!" Nape swore. He was a lot more at home on his feet than he was on a horse. The huntsman lit a stout tar torch and entered the cavern. Ned and the pack's other lead dog Bolt kept close to their master's side. Cu'chulain had seen them and crept on to a higher ledge, scaling a sheer side of rock face, until he was in striking distance of the bats hanging from the roof. There he waited.

Inspired by the lead dogs and their master, other hounds followed them into the pothole. The echoing tumult of the dogs sent the bats near Cu'chulain's head flitting through the air. Their loud shrieks grated in his ears. Josiah Nape lowered his torch so that the flame illuminated his face in a Hallowe'en mask. He fired his rifle from the hip into the ceiling, where he had seen the movement of the bats. The shot narrowly missed Cu'chulain's head, but his cunning and nerve kept him poised like something frozen in time. The hairs on the back of his neck bristled with wrath and fright. Seeing no response to his shot except for the torment of the bats, Nape signalled to his dogs to move out. They waded back towards the entrance. Cu'chulain had seen them and was slinking along the cave wall, springing from one jutting rock to another. He was now following the two lead hounds, Ned and Bolt, and the huntsman away from the cave.

The tables were now turned. The man was on his own behind his hounds and Cu'chulain could smell the stink of his fear. He stalked him along the side of the stream, as Nape fell further and further behind his dogs. His musket had been fired. Unaware, he carried it unloaded as a club. Cu'chulain sneaked through the grass and the mud, his tail swaying for balance. As long as there was noise from the hounds upstream, he knew that the man could not hear him coming. When the barking and splashing stopped, he stayed still. He grew bolder as he inched closer to the noise of the man pushing through the stream.

The shadow of his enemy began to stir his torments. In the blinking of his eyes, he saw flashes of hands brandishing clubs and opening cage doors, and weals and wounds from sword and whip. Cu'chulain narrowed his eyes so that they were now squinting at the moving shape. His big tail switched, held just above the grass, and his claws dug into the damp earth on the bank. His tiger stripes swelled as his skin crawled with the smell of vengeance. Nape might as well have had a sheep's liver strapped to his head. Cu'chulain watched his prey tremble without his hounds. He could hear Nape talking to himself, as he made for the opposite bank. He kept looking behind him but did not see Cu'chulain whose stripes blended with the grass. "Nay, bloody hell, where are those dogs? They must've caught scent of fox. There may be deer up there and all. Aye, that be it. That will be the reason."

The man's fear leaked into the air. Cu'chulain's jaw muscles tightened. He began to yawn in a threat. He sloped into the burn some fifty yards away from Josiah Nape. The coolness of the water rushed past his chest, sometimes breaking a little higher up to his neck. His pointer was his hot lathered red tongue, hanging limp out of the side of his jaw. He salivated as he closed in on Nape. Although the huntsman was large, surprise was with the tiger wolf. The hairs on the back of the man's neck stood up as he shivered. As he turned round expecting to see a ghost, he saw a blur as the beast broke out of the water with a giant leap. Screaming in fright, the grey huntsman dropped his musket into the water. The tiger wolf smacked into his chest, knocking him backwards into the stream. And so floundering under the rush of the stream, Nape's fight for life began. He could not find his footing, since the rocks were slippery. Here the tiger wolf had the advantage, as he seemed to paw the water itself, levering his lesser weight against his quarry. As Nape's face rose up through the breaking waters, it was met by the open mouth of the beast, which snapped at his features, drawing blood from the man's jowls. But there was no time to tear, for Nape disappeared once more under the water, just as one of the straggling foxhounds showed its head over the top of the bank.

Pulling back from the huntsman, Cu'chulain leapt from the water to get rid of the dog as quickly as possible, as though it were the witness of a crime. The foxhound turned, but before it had time to bolt, Cu'chulain had dragged it by its hind quarters, howling into the stream, where he killed it as easily as one of the ewes. The body pumped blood into the current, clouding the crystal waters. Then the beast turned back to its lair.

Josiah Nape was wounded, but not dead. He sat up in a shallow part of the stream and stared at the back of the tiger wolf. "May God, saints preserve us. 'Tis a tiger or a lion." He put his hand to the side of his face and plunged his fingers into the furrow that had opened from his ear to his chin. Looking around him, he saw a cloud of blood staining the stream as it flowed from the side of his face and mingled with the blood of his hound. He pulled out his handkerchief and staunched his gaping wound. He rose, pushing through the water to the bank, and strode over the dead foxhound, before squelching onto the grass with his high riding boots.

Spotting a couple of huntsmen approaching on horseback, Nape waved frantically with his free hand. "Help!" he cried. They had found his horse, which had run off with the hounds.

"Well, lads," Nape slurred, "ye best get me back to the doctor's and have him stitch me up." He slumped quietly to his knees, as if he had come to pray. The huntsmen dismounted and drew closer to Nape. They were bewildered by their master's foul wound. "Tis a girt lion we seek, I'm sure of it," Nape said. His men said nothing and helped him back onto his feet. His horse was brought forward, and he was helped into the saddle, blood still running down his hand on to his grey kit and dripped quietly onto the saddle.

MATILDA Dagobert was shaking fine sand from a silver holder to blot a letter, when suddenly she went rigid. Below her the slaves were complaining again. The sound was as a sea wind mingled with the voice of Potter's hunters. They moaned in low monotones and their manacles clattered and clinked as they shifted in fear and doubt of what would become of them. Lady Dagobert rang the silver bell on her writing desk, its little tinkle lost in the melancholy and the shaking of the fetters from below. The great lady felt her hair prickle under her wig, while a mouse shivered up her spine. "Bah!" She sat straight on her stool. "As if these blacks would scare me." The butler brought in her estate manager, who was ready to transport the slaves immediately. "You'd better make haste, Mister Curwen. I do not want my cargo wasting away en route. And there is a long journey to the Carolinas. They will fetch a considerable sum there or on the block at the Charleston Auction."

Thomas Curwen bowed and replied, "As you wish, my lady." He knew not to question her decision to bring the journey a day forward. He also knew that to leave now would make the journey more perilous. Even as the slaves were being herded in front of the drawing-room window for her to view, they continued to sing. One after the other they joined in chanting the songs of their fathers. And beyond the gates of Clifton Hall, they carried on their chants of pain and woe. But now the hunters were defiant in their silence.

So began their long march along the coastal road to Morecambe Bay and then to Lancaster. There were at least forty men treading in single file. Old potato sacks gave them little cover against the harsh West Cumbrian elements. Their hoods made them look like dark monks on a long pilgrimage. The main overseer kept them in line, cracking his whip as they went, while the slaves wailed the songs of their ancestors to seek their protection. The other overseers smoked clay pipes on their saddles, every now and again spitting tobacco juice into the path of the slaves.

"C'mon, ye devils," sneered the boss man. "Ye'll soon be ready to march across bay." Oblivious to his words, the hunters and slaves kept moving, their hard feet padding on the limestone gravel and chains clanging as they went.

LADY Dagobert was duly informed that the master of the Melbreak Hunt had been badly hurt by the monster of a creature that ripped hounds and ewes to pieces and drank their blood. When the old matriarch arrived at the temporary clinic in the rear of the Punch Bowl public house, she was very low. The wounds on her legs were beginning to heal, but they had taken the heat out of the aged firebrand. She tottered through the rear door of the public house, followed by her black house servant, both crowned by white powdered wigs. She was still furious that she had to lower herself by coming here, for Josiah Nape had refused to come to Clifton Hall. But she was eager, in spite of this, to inspect the huntsman's injuries at close quarters.

Nape had been stitched up very carefully. What with the bruising and forty-seven large stitches, he looked like the monster from the novel *Frankenstein* she had just read by that odious Mary Shelley. Lady Dagobert said nothing, but she scented a whiff from the bottles of grog Nape had consumed to take away the pain of Doctor Todhunter's work.

"Have you been drinking, Mister Nape?" she asked.

"Aye, of course I bloody well have, yer Ladyship," Nape growled. "I just narrowly missed having me throat torn out!"

Matilda Dagobert was prepared for his directness. "Tell me, Mister Nape," she said, "did you see what this banshee that carved you up looked like?"

"In my mind, yer Ladyship, t'was some kind of great lion. Or one of those tigers. Them beasts they's bringing back from India."

"Of course it's not a lion or a tiger, you fool! That one has been dealt with! No, Mister Nape, it is something quite different. I know where it's come from. It is the same one that killed my brave dogs at Whitehaven two weeks ago!" She looked faint, and she held out her hand to her servant as if she needed steadying. He stepped forward and gently supported her lower arm. She took a deep breath and resumed. "Mister Nape, I shall pay your medical fee myself. And I must let you know that I shall be calling upon Mister John Peel. In your absence from the field, it is only right that he himself should carry on the pursuit of this terrible quarry."

"Aye, yer Ladyship, well, good luck to him," Nape replied. "I have never come across anything like this before."

"Good day to you, sir," she said, and she was helped over the threshold of the public house on to the dirt track where her carriage was waiting. When she was settled in it, she peered through the window at the frontage of the public house as if it were filth. Then she brought out a fan from inside her coat sleeve and opened it to cool herself. "Drive on!" she barked. As the horses strained forward, she was thrown back into her velvet seat, where she rocked with the buck and jerk of the iron-rimmed wheels.

11

"Do ye think them blacks would like to get their hands dirty down there and do some real work for me with that lot?" The fisherman pointed out over the great expanse of tawny sand. "See them specks on horizon? Well, there's three dozen men there picking cockles, and some of them tending the fish traps. What do ye say, ganger? Can we borrow them men for a couple of days to work the cockles?"

Lady Dagobert's overseer dismounted from his horse. "Aye, get me sack, would ye?" he said. "Nay's the answer. One job, one life, that's all I have got."

The fisherman took his hat off. "Well, ye could make yourself a few guineas before ye reach Lancaster. I have a load of shellfish out on the sands that need humped back onto the jetty.

"Nay, sir," the overseer said. "We just wait here for sand pilot."

"Well, please yourself, 'tis your loss." The fisherman disappeared down on to the shore, where a horse and cart was ready and waiting for him. As the cart moved out on to the shore, so the sand pilot, who would take the slaves across the bay to Lancaster, came apace. He was a tall rangy man wearing an old sou'wester and leather breeches. He wore two pistols on his side, which hung in pirate fashion from crossed bucklers. He introduced himself to the overseer. "Well, now, an interesting cargo ye have there."

The overseer rooted in his saddlebags for some coinage. "I have been instructed to give ye this fee from Lady Dagobert. Half now, and half when we reach other side."

The sand pilot reached out his hand for the leather sack. After he'd rummaged about in it, he raised his hand to his sou'wester and tugged it. "Thankee," he said.

"Right, let's be sending them along. We do not want to be caught by the tide, do we?"

One of the armed guards, who was with the overseer, leant forward on his steed. "They tell me the tide moves as fast as a galloping horse on them sands. That be right, sand pilot?"

"Aye, that's about right. Be better for them black lads if we got horses then? We shall probably get to see the coach somewhere down there. Finest geldings in the country drawing the mail, ye know."

"Right, come on, let's move."

The dark figures stepped down onto the shore. They winced as the cold northerly breeze hit them. The larger hunters hung their heads, except for Suniman, who eyed Lady Dagobert's guards from behind his sack cowl. The last of the guards pushed his musket butt into Suniman's shoulders, urging him forward. Reluctant at first, he began to stride out over the sands. Soon the small seaport of Silverdale was disappearing into the distance, as the groups of men with their cargo of slaves dwindled away on the first part of their journey across the bay.

AS Lady Dagobert's coach drew near to a copse of woodland, fringed by a lakeland stone wall, a tall man emerged from the shadows of the trees. He sat solid astride his mount, a familiar dun coloured fell pony. He wore the standard grey livery of the Lakeland huntsmen, not the scarlet coats of the gentry. He was not alone. As was his custom, he was followed by his faithful pack of hunting terriers, coupled with chains. The coachman reined in the horses before the copse. By this time, Matilda Dagobert was peering out. "Is he here?" she shouted to her coachman.

"Yes, ma'am," he replied. "He has arrived."

"Good, good. Bring him to me. I want to see him."

With a white-gloved hand, the coachman beckoned the tall man. The huntsman cantered down towards the carriage, followed by his terriers. He kept control of them by swishing at them with his crop. The dowager watched his horse's head nod and move past the coach window, as John Peel stooped slightly so that he could see into the carriage.

"Yer ladyship asked for this meeting, so I came immediately. I have brought me boys to see ye." He gestured towards the pack at his back.

"Thank you, sir," Lady Dagobert replied, raising herself out of the velvet seat and squinting at the huntsman's infamous terriers. "I see they are all sharp set and hungry," she said.

"We have been breeding new blood into them, me lady. A very hard type of box-headed dog I've come to know. Some Irish brought them into Cleator Moor. They call them red devils. Dead game and iron hard."

"Well, at least the Irish are bringing something good to the Lake District, sir. Damn their Fenian hides."

Peel continued, "I have talked to Josiah Nape, ma'am, and I heard tell of this strange animal ye have charged me to be rid of. We need some bull terrier bred dogs to cope with this." He looked at Lady Dagobert with his piercing blue eyes. "Shall we call it a wolf or a dog, me lady? They tell that this animal savaged yer mastiffs."

The dowager's white face began to redden, and she replied, "It always amazes me how news of defeat travels faster than news of victory. You should know, sir, that I shall bring this animal to heel as I shall bring to heel its master. I am giving a bounty on this beast's head. A substantial sum of money. Five hundred guineas."

Peel was not a rich man. He turned his head in the direction of the failing sun. "I shall do my best, my lady. I have taken the liberty of calling some of my colleagues with their hunting dogs to take part. We meet in twenty-four hours time at Ennerdale stone circle."

"I will be there, sir. For the stirrup cup."

"Nay, we will be on foot."

Turning away from Peel, Lady Dagobert said, "Coachman, drive back to Clifton Hall." The carriage set off, leaving Peel and his eight red dogs behind the wheels of the hansom.

ALL the time the hooded slave procession moved forward, the sand pilot moved nimbly in front, looking across the mud for signs of the treacherous sinking sand for which the bay was notorious. He carried with him stick fronds, and when there was a dangerous place to be avoided, he left a marker. They approached the mixed company of cocklers and fishermen, all grubbing in the sand with jumbos to ease the cockles to the surface. But the men had to work in a lather, rocking the boards back and forth to find the shellfish. Every so often a man, caked in his own sweat, would rest. Occasionally, they would look up briefly from the raking to see the slaves looking back at them.

This provoked insults of, "Black continent's not in this county, lads!" or "and ye might be finding a gibbet at Lancaster. They already hung a couple of yer kind just this last week!" The slaves showed no emotion, for they did not understand the jibes and taunts of the fisherman, only their contempt. The overseers and armed guards grinned and made a show of their authority over the slaves. One guard cantered up to Suniman and kicked him in the side. Suniman took the blow without flinching, but his eyes were hot with anger. The overseer and the armed guards had now stopped, as they traded news with the fishermen and cocklers. The slaves stood and looked around the melancholy sands.

"Tell Lady Dagobert," the fisherman said, "if there's work going on up at her estate, there's a couple of lads down here with good records."

"Aye, well, ye know what jobs are like on her estate," replied the overseer, looking directly at the fisherman. "They're like rocking horse shite." There was laughter and guffaws from the white men.

Suniman thought that they were mocking him and the other slaves. He could take no more. Seeing that the sand pilot was a few hundred yards ahead, he decided to make a fight of it. He gently tugged the chains of the man attached to him. This signal was relayed down the line, while the white men laughed on. Suniman shrugged off his hood with his shoulders. The slaves launched themselves in their chains at their captors. An armed guard managed to fire a shot into the air, but it had no effect. The band of hunters and slaves dragged the main overseer off his horse and into the sand, raining blows on his stubbly face until he was unconscious. On his belt, Suniman saw the keys. He picked them up and began to open the locks.

One of the armed guards had had enough and galloped his horse back in the direction of Silverdale. The other armed guards aimed their pistols at the slaves and fired at random, but once free of their bonds, the slaves turned on them. They stormed the men on the horses, dragging mount and rider into the sand. The fishermen and cocklers gathered in a tight bunch of two dozen men. They gawped at the three dozen enraged slaves. The fisherman's leader stood before his men.

"Will ye stand by and watch this affront while our cousins from Cumberland are killed?" he cried. "My God, ye heathens, ye shall swing at Lancaster Castle for this!"

Suniman and the other hunters stretched themselves to their full height and glared at the men they thought had mocked them. Tightly packed, they crossed the cockle beds to where the fishermen and cocklers stood. The two groups squared up to each other on the rippled sands under the cold blue sky of Morecambe Bay. The cocklers and fishermen carried knives and billy clubs and other tools of their trade. Where they had been working, the sand was mushy and great sacks of shellfish lay strewn about. From the rear of the cocklers, a man shouted, "If we want to give them blackies a hiding, we better be sharpish. I think the bloody tide's about to turn!"

Another shouted, "C'mon, lads, let's get into them!"

As they moved forward, the slaves began to sing in deep and tremulous tones. Their war chant was chilling. The white men lost their nerve. Another cockler shouted, "Eh, well, I have me wife and babbies to think about." Dropping his tools, he headed back over the sands in the direction of Silverdale.

Yet another cockler piped up, "Well, we must get back, or the tide'll be at us." Two more moved quickly away from the rest of the group, but still the hunters and the slaves moved closer. "Looks like we are outnumbered, Jack."

"Well, it is looking that way, ain't it?" said another.

One by one, the cocklers and fishermen were turning and walking away, stopping only to rescue the unconscious guards and the dead overseer from the incoming tide. Suniman halted his men with an outstretched hand. They began to sing a chant of victory. The aggressive ganger looked back and shouted, "Right, ye sons of bitches, we'll tell the militia when we get back. Ye'll all be dead men at Lancaster."

The sand pilot was heading towards the middle of the bay, marking the route with birch fronds in between the treacherous quicksands. He was nothing but a speck on the horizon. Suniman looked about where the fight with the overseer had taken place. Scattered on the ground were the man's belongings, a pistol, a pouch of tobacco and some other items. Suniman pointed towards the things, and one of the other slaves picked them up. The fleeing white men grew smaller as they reached the mainland. Now Suniman pointed in the direction of the tiny figure of the sand pilot.

The slaves and hunters made across the sands on their own. They ran towards the sand pilot with a sense of rhythm. Some of them threw away their sack clothing as they went. The group slowed down as they saw a birch frond waving in the wind in the sand. They were on the right track. Suniman brushed it with his hand and they carried on. After about another mile, they picked up another frond, but it was on the banks of a great channel of water. The hunters and slaves were fearful, as the sea was troubled and rising quickly. But the big hunter forged on, jumping into the fast-running tide. The waters came up to his chest, as he part walked and part swam across the channel. In the middle the water had moved down his body so that there was surf around his midriff, and the other men pitched into the river and followed him.

Wearing only the remnants of their sack clothing over their glistening flesh, they climbed out on the opposite bank. They were barely in time. Had they delayed, the waters would have been too deep to cross. The sand pilot was now clearly visible some half a mile away. The Africans carried on through the quicksands and the channels of rising water. They went past mussel beds that would have cut their bare feet to slices and on towards Bolton-le-Sands on the far side.

Suniman turned to look back. Where there had been sands was now covered with the tide, which had come swirling in behind them. They were now in a race against the rising waters of the bay. They ran on at an increased pace. The clouds above had thicken and the wind was blowing against the sides of the slaves. The sand pilot was like a will-o-the-wisp, darting here and there across the beach and every so often sticking in a frond of birch. The runaway slaves pursued him relentlessly, but the tide was lapping at their heels, drawing level with them on either side, so that they were constantly under the threat of being cut off and drowned.

The wind was raising up spray from the sand and blowing it at the fugitives, their smooth black faces now raw from the cold salt air. Suniman shouted something in his native tongue to the sand pilot. He then looked round to see one of the straggling slaves waving his hands in the air. The tide had caught him. He was the first to be dragged under the surface. Nobody stopped. They ran on with their sack cloths flapping behind them, some of them crying into the whistle of the gusts. Their feet slapped on the damp ribs of sand. Soon they were running through salt water. The tiny hamlet of Bolton-le-Sands nestled safely on the other side, but they were tiring. The sand pilot seemed to stop, but then he moved on again. Suniman grasped another birch frond as if it were a mercy, now that they faced a watery death. The men pushed on through the spume, which was now swirling round their knees under the now formidable skies. Some of the men in the rear were now up to their waists in the cold grey tide.

The sand pilot turned and came back towards them. He could not bear their pitiful cries any longer. Suniman forged ahead with two of his hunters. The sand pilot was pointing in the direction of a small mound of dry sand. Suniman could see this, and he shouted at his men to make for the bank. They dragged themselves from the waters and climbed the mound, but they were now encircled by sea. The sand pilot took off his sou'wester and threw it into the sand.

"I can do no more for ye!" he cried. "I shall be caught myself! I never seen the tide run so fast!" And away he went.

Suniman made for the small river, which the tide was filling quickly, and he leapt in, followed by the two other hunters. But, while he clambered up the riverbank, they were swept away. To his horror, he saw his men bobbing about on the water like buoys. One by one, they began to disappear. Some of them clawed at the air above them, looking for a lifeline to grip, as the fierce current underneath them sucked them below.

Suniman pulled his way up the bank until he was out of the water, apart from his thighs. Lapsing in and out of consciousness, he could feel the rising tide moving up past his buttocks into the small of his back, its coldness trying to drag him down. He clawed on, raking his fingers through the sand as he pulled his large body up and out, giving himself time to lie until the tide licked at his feet, and he had to move again. Even Suniman's two finest hunters had been swept away. Now he was alone. As he crawled towards the shale and stones of Bolton-le-Sands, he was met by a small crowd of sombre men and women. A round lady with a ruddy complexion put a pillow of cloth under his head and gave him a drink of honey and whisky.

"Thou poor lost soul," she said. "Washed up by the tide onto the shore.

From whence canst thou have come?"

Suniman tried to form a word in his native tongue, but he fell into unconsciousness. The lady turned to the others and said, "We must get him to a hearth. A desperate cold runs through his body. Almighty God has summoned us here to bring him in to our midst and to take care of him."

Two of the brethren stooped to lift Suniman off the sand. One of them said, "Sister, the Lord God has brought unto us a lost brother. We must teach him the ways of the Lord."

The sand pilot approached the Quaker brethren, his sou'wester still dripping with the salt water from the bay. From behind the shoulders of the dark-clad gathering, he made his confession. "He is the only one out of two dozen slaves to have lived. I have taken payment and not fulfilled my side of the bargain. Instead I saved myself. I have sinned in the eyes of the Lord."

The Quakers turned to face the sand pilot, their faces solemn. One of the older men approached him and said, "Indeed thou hast, if this be so. Go down on your knees and beg the Lord's forgiveness. We shall help you steer clear of the gates of Satan."

His hands trembling, the sand pilot took out the purse containing half of his arranged fee, and he handed it to the elder. "Please give him this. 'Twill pay for his restoration."

The elder took the purse and smiled. "Praise be. For Judas has returned the silver. And so saved his soul."

The sand pilot fell to his knees on the shale, and the whole gathering exclaimed, "Praise the Lord!"

12

Cu'chulain cavorted like a naughty puppy that had been stealing sausages. He was running and spinning in the grass, sometimes stopping suddenly to roll and scrape his striped body on the damp earth. He clawed at the ground, kicking lumps of grass into the air. When his play was done, he went further upstream and drank, lapping the water into his mouth. His stream seemed far from man, and he roamed its banks, an open artery of the land like those of the dead sheep. To live at all needed the flow of blood or water.

Long ago, as far as people could remember, the dog and the wolf had been worshipped by hunters and farmers who lived off the land. Local tribes had thrown offerings of bronze dogs and wolves into the river, and they who put their life force into the soil were given it back in meat and milk. Now the tiger wolf had come to the sacred ground of the fells to remind them. He scented the air. The smell of animals and humans was drifting from the valley below, where the new meet was being organised. He lolloped on a little faster, his muscular body pushing on through the mud and the fading grasslands, his keen eyes ever intent against the threat massing below at Brig House.

A MILE further down the valley, an army of terriers, hounds, horses and men were gathering at the mysterious monoliths of the ancient stone circle with its pagan traditions. The first of the fell packs to arrive was the Melbreak Hunt. The master of the hounds and all his whippers-in were dressed in red coats. They were closely followed by their foxhounds, which had been sharp set to make them zealous in their pursuit of the beast. They barked savagely as they led the huntsmen into the stone circle. The master blew on his brass horn, which sounded like the trumpets of the armies of Israel bringing down the walls of Jericho.

A group of specialist hunters now appeared on foot with their heavy long-legged wolfhounds. Since the last wolf had been killed in a cave further down the coast a hundred years before, these dogs had been trained to kill the red deer of the Lake District. They were followed from the east by the Ennerdale Hunt, the hounds baying so loudly that the tumult seemed to echo around all of West Cumbria. The long whips of the men in grey could not quiet the racket of the dogs, mad to go after the biggest game of all. Much of the discussion revolved around the old witch woman in the next valley, who could make the circle hum by waving the whiskers of a black cat. Drunken revellers would go there at the summer solstice to listen to the stones sigh and breathe. They would swear they could hear the voices of their ancestors. Perhaps people and animals had been sacrificed on the huge stone in the middle of the circle. Their blood had flowed into channels in the rock, only to be poured back into the land.

Lady Dagobert rattled towards the meet in the luxury of her coach, drawn by horses sporting crimson plumes. She now had two coachmen instead of one, and the second servant was armed with a blunderbuss. Lady Dagobert's stick figure jogged on the velvet seats. Every so often she raised her hands to her head to adjust her powdered wig like Marie Antoinette, although she did not intend to lose her head. She carried with her a recent letter from her nephew William Hackett.

My dearest Aunt,

I am happy to inform you that the pirate ship the Great Michael was sighted in the Pacific Ocean some weeks ago by the King's vessel, a frigate called the Penelope. As this vessel is now condemned for piracy, it will please you to know that there will be more ships from the King's Navy pursuing these outlaws.   *Your obedient servant,*

William, Carlisle Castle, 12th October 1810

The embittered old dowager saw that the meet was as vibrant as her enemy Potter's menagerie. Steam rose into the air above the stone circle, spouting from the cauldron of milling people who gathered in a violent heaving as hot bubbles bursting. The dogs were scenting the beast.

Two gallant whippers-in from the Melbreak Hunt walked over and escorted Lady Dagobert's coach into the perimeter of the stone circle. A coachman jumped down from his seat and opened the carriage door, from where she emerged unassisted to sit on a wooden stool. The masters of the hunt fawned around her, taking off their hats and saluting her. The dogs snapped and howled so loudly that they had to move close to Lady Dagobert to hear her words of vengeance. She summoned up her strength and spoke clearly, "Whosoever shall kill this beast that has so affronted everything we stand for – and which has cost me a small fortune – shall be rewarded with the sum of five hundred guineas for its hide. Or whatever proof remains of its death."

A tall gaunt figure stepped out from the shadow of a great standing stone. The most famous of the huntsmen came over to where the masters were listening to the vengeful matriarch. "We shall not fail ye, ma'am," John Peel said. "'Tis no different from a fox, only bigger. Josiah Nape has already driven it to ground. This is the pledge of John Peel. This fiend shall be nailed either this day or the next. I shall not rest 'til I bring ye its tail."

Lady Dagobert nodded her approval and then glared at her coachman to open the coach door. He assisted her into the carriage, climbed back into his seat and whipped the horses back to Clifton Hall.

CU'CHULAIN was drinking from the river and feeding from a sheep he had killed earlier. Drawn curiously closer to the danger brewing at the stone circle, he crawled stealthily through the brown bracken, his guts as coiled iron springs. He yawned at the menace to come. Already there were men loose on the hills with their killer coursing dogs. Here he skulked, waiting to attack any unwary straggler.

His first kill came quickly. A young man had slipped his lurcher off its lead to bound through the heather and bracken towards where Cu'chulain bided his time in the undergrowth. He gripped the lurcher's neck and with one turn of his body, he throttled the dog's bark, crushed its windpipe and cracked its sinews. Leaving the dying dog, Cu'chulain sprung out of his hiding place. He brought down the young lad, who had never seen any quarry larger than a fox or a deer in his life. The lad screamed once before being brought low for the beast to tear out his throat. His blood was bitter to Cu'chulain's tongue.

The beast now struck out towards the stone circle, where the group of huntsmen and dogs had now begun the chase. With John Peel sounding his horn to signal that the hunt was on, the bloodthirsty horde of men and dogs set off towards the fells. From high on the ridge above the stream, Cu'chulain loped on towards the stone circle. His cunning had enabled him to be downwind of the scenting dogs. He swung on, avoiding the areas where the men had stood. He could see the fog of their wrath, the smell of their anger. In his eyes, the hunters at the great stone lair had retreated because of his advance. Creeping through the bracken closer to where the men on foot were standing, he began to stalk the last of the hounds. He saw them as the weak ones, who could not keep up with the pack. A red mist covered his sight, and he began to drool.

Nose wet and ears pricked up, he sniffed at the sharp scent of fright. Then he was thundering through the bracken. Using his tail to balance his charge, he gaped his huge jaws and another man was dead before his well fed body hit the heather. Cu'chulain had ripped out his throat with one tug and then leapt off his chest. His hunting partner was crying, "Jesus, Mary and Joseph! That's no dog, that's a great lion!" He aimed at the myth with his pistol. There was a flash and a bang, but the ball was well wide of its target.

Several of the large hunting dogs scarpered. Their whelps of fear jittered back and echoed round the stone circle. Yet through the coarse undergrowth stormed several terriers, released by an old man who had watched the scene from a distance. Bred as stayers, these dogs were hard and game and would never back down.

The first of the wire-haired terriers was caught mid-air in the gulf of the tiger wolf's jaws and flung up. It landed sprawling. The wind was knocked out of it, but it was up again. Cu'chulain turned his head quickly to protect his flanks from the onslaught of the terriers with his teeth, trying to grip their fur in death locks. There were five dogs hanging from his rear and tail like biting burrs, but he could not get at them. The old man lifted his musket, but his terriers were in the way of his aim. With his Herculean strength, Cu'chulain clambered along the ground, dragging the dogs behind him.

Wallowing from side to side under the immense strain, he made for the sacrificial slab in the middle of the stone circle. He began to squash two of the terriers against the granite, squeezing the life out of them now that they were trapped, although the other three dogs still tugged at his flesh. Once they had fallen off his body, Cu'chulain climbed upon the stone, his claws leaving scratch marks on its rough face. Now he dumped down on his other flank, mashing the terriers beneath. Then he sprang to his feet and crushed their heads with scissor bites. The last terrier got up. Its fearless courage would not let it run. But by the time the demented old man opened fire on the beast, it was dropping over the back of the sacrificial altar and snaking through the grass. Far away over the hills, the horde of men and dogs were charging to no purpose.

Cu'chulain was not finished. Instead of skulking off, he turned to face the old man and his empty gun. The man's fear stank. Four of his terriers were dead and the fifth, though cut and slashed, just stood and barked. Narrowing his black eyes, Cu'chulain snarled. The old man had never seen the like of this. Now he tasted the fear he had thrust on other animals through his dogs. Cu'chulain crept closer. Just as he got within striking distance, the blood drained from the old man's face, his knees buckled, and he collapsed to the ground as a corn sack. The shock had stopped his heart dead.

Cu'chulain moved closer to the fallen man and began to sniff the new corpse. His burning eyes had dulled. His wet black nose explored one of the old man's pockets and pulled out pieces of cheese meant as rewards for the terriers. Cu'chulain then cocked his leg and pissed on the old man's shoes. He gulped down the cheese and turned to run with a steady gait out of the stone circle, ignoring the wounded terrier by the sacrificial stone. Cu'chulain sensed that his enemies were now in retreat. He smelt man and dog fear everywhere. He was driven on in the pursuit of his pursuers by the angry red mist that filled his brain and scent glands.

Half way up Ennerdale Fell, the hunt was in full cry. John Peel led the way, flanked by the masters of the Melbreak and Ennerdale Hunts. All three men were grim as they urged on the dogs. The packs had now mingled into one as two shades of paint. The purer Ennerdale foxhounds had browner and more ginger coats than the lighter coloured and more versatile Melbreak pack. "Yut, yut, yut!" Peel shouted at the top of his voice among the barking and snarling of the dogs in their fury. About a quarter of a mile behind them, the shorter terriers were finding it hard to keep sight of the foxhounds. They too had their masters, who followed on fell ponies. As the great spectacle unfolded over the West Cumbrian landscape, any wild animal was now fair game. Red deer were driven from hiding in the small forests encircling the fell by the foxhounds, who pulled them down, only to be lashed back by their whippers-in. The deer were dispatched by single ball shot, to be picked up at a later date.

Cu'chulain was dogging the thrash up the side of the fell. He ran along the sides of slate stone walls through burns and copses, leaping over fences on the scent of the fear ahead to reach the straggling smaller game dogs. The beast was catching up with the great hunt. Peel held up his hand with authority, and the hunters mustered round him. He knew something was wrong. The foxhounds checked, looking up at their masters. "We have no spoor!" Peel said. "The dogs are taking other game. They know the smell of this creature. Though they be sharp set, they have not taken." His penetrating gaze challenged the other huntsmen to say otherwise, but there was no answer.

Further down the fell side, the terrier men and their dogs were breaking from the bracken. The dogs were small enough not to be seen rustling their way through it. Cu'chulain had stayed ready to strike at this rear guard of the main force of dogs. Now he brazenly clambered onto a large outcrop of rock on the flank of the men on their ponies. As the first of several men appeared below him, Cu'chulain leapt from the rock and unhorsed the king of the terrier men. His pony bolted, frightened and kicking out its back hooves, while Cu'chulain crushed the man's jaw and left him for dead.

This surprise attack scattered the others. Their faces were white and empty with shock and horror, as Cu'chulain drifted back up the rock face, until he stood proud on his perch, an icon of cunning and courage. The men got a good view of the creature from its striped coat and its muscular flanks to its hyena head, broad across the eyes and wide across its great jaws.

"Feckit and dammit!" one of the men cursed.

The terriers swarmed from the bracken and tried to climb the rock on which the beast stood, like imps scaling the stronghold of Satan. Cu'chulain kept his eye on the men. The shock of the slaying of their leader was wearing off, and they were reaching for their guns. Just as a couple of the terriers began to snap at his paws, Cu'chulain turned and began climbing higher into the rocks, using his claws as clamps. He heard the whistle of the ball, as one of the men let loose, but missed him.

The blast carried up the side of the fell, and Peel turned. He took out a small spyglass from his lapel pocket and scanned bracken. "God Christ!" he muttered under his breath, as he spotted the leader of the terrier men sprawled out dead. The rest of his company looked as if they were forming a firing squad for an execution. Then Peel saw the beast, hemmed into a high crevice and out of firing range. He swallowed and gagged, although he showed no other sign of fear. The other master huntsmen stopped dead and waited for their orders. Peel pointed at the facing mountainside, until the huntsmen saw what was in view. Peel screamed, "Yut, yut, yut! C'mon, boys! There's blood in the air!" And away they went, howling like banshees down the fellside to the corpse.

Peel stood over his dead colleague, his face blue from being throttled by the beast. The rest of the huntsmen gathered round to gawp. The hounds swirled around them and tried to climb the steep face of the rock, where Cu'chulain was trapped. He yawned in defiance again and again. He seemed always ready to pounce, putting one claw forward onto the dark slate, while he continued to scan the hordes of grey and the hounds. Then he pulled back, leaping on to a higher perch. Peel predicted his next move. "This cunning one will scale the rock face and make for the top of the fell," he said. "Then 'tis clear in the open ground with a head start." The whippers-in nodded, while Peel directed his attention to the terrier men. "Let us hope this death has made ye hot to kill this monster. Tak yer dogs and climb. Get as high as ye can. We will meet it on the far side." He took off his black hunting cap and cried, "Ho! To the far side of Ennerdale!"

The further up the cliffside he climbed, the more Cu'chulain smelt the sea air. When he came to a narrow cleft, he was able to sidle in among the shale. Yet he was beginning to tire from his efforts in these confined and unnatural spaces. So when his paws reached the grasses again, he sped into the open countryside and down Ennerdale Fell. His instinct was to wear down his prey over distance, and he could lope as far as the horizon. Peel was deluded into thinking the beast was running away, while it was choosing the ground on which to make a stand against the horde set against it. The scent of water took Cu'chulain towards the River Esket. Meanwhile, the terrier men had stuffed their dogs into open sacks to carry them up the rock face. Wearing sturdy clogs to protect their feet, each man helped the other, their numb hands grasping the natural holds in the rock.

Peel and the Ennerdale and Melbreak huntsmen burst out of the boulders round the far side of Ennerdale Fell. They could see the track of the beast, for it put up every pheasant and partridge on its way through the bracken. Cu'chulain crouched, panting to cool himself and shaking his head from side to side. While his underbelly pressed into the dank earth, the hunt got closer, with the lead hounds from both packs forging ahead of the huntsmen. Three of the lead dogs were first to reach Cu'chulain. Two of them charged past, while the third came face to face with him. From his low lie in the grass, he opened his wide jaws and locked on to the head of the foxhound, flipping it over and breaking its neck. By the time the hunters caught up, all they could see was their dead hound in the bracken. The ferocity of the attacks from a single predator kept the packs of dogs from attacking straight away. Instead they circled, bayed and snarled.

Cu'chulalin turned on a groat to meet another strike. He leapt on one of the two huntsmen who were crawling for cover, biting off his ear and ripping the flesh from one side of his face. Both of them were screaming, and Peel was yelling uselessly. But the hounds were growing bolder. They started to snap at the creature and, when they could not get at it, they started on each other. And so the packs began to fight their fellow dogs, while Cu'chulain vanished like a phantom. By the time he decided to make for water, he had killed seven hounds, hardly used to pursuing something that fought back, red in tooth and claw.

The demonic terriers had slipped from their leashes and were now pelting through the bracken towards Cu'chulain. Peel knew that a pronged attack from them could be a problem for the creature. Then in a thunderbolt he remembered what Josiah Nape had told him - the beast was attracted to water. He raced down to the river to hem him in, while the dogs were still in hot pursuit. Peel made for the shallows, just as Cu'chulain reached the banks on the other side of the river. The huntsman drew his pistol, sighted the creature and fired a lead ball.

When the shot ripped into his side, Cu'chulain did not make a sound. How could such teeth hurt from so far? A red hot sear scorched his guts, and before he had time to leap into the river, the terriers had caught him, hanging from his stripes like clothes pegs. Twisting and writhing in the grass, Cu'chulain tore back at them with his teeth. He tugged them off and tossed them up like rags, but still they kept on biting. The flame in his ribs made him yearn for the coolness that only the water could give. So he leapt into the bend of the river. Only two terriers now remained, and they had taken hold of his flanks. Panting, Cu'chulain kept his head up. The terriers dropped off to stop themselves drowning and paddled for the shore. To the astonishment of the huntsmen, the creature swam in a circle to face its persecutors once more.

Peel's gaze fixed on the beast, which looked back. Cu'chulain kicked in the bloodshot water, making for the bank. By now, the pack had come up, their ears falling forward and their necks stretched to get at the tiger wolf. The dogs in the rear were pushing those at the front into the water, cheered on by Peel. Cu'chulain strove towards the clay bank, where he faced the pack of hounds. But still those jaws opened wide, tearing and biting any hound that came near, until the weight of the pack pressing down forced him onto his flank. Now half a dozen terriers tormented him and bloody strips of flesh criss-crossed the stripes on his fur.

Torn to shreds, Cu'chulain yawned in defiance for one last time. And then he was dead. Two of the huntsmen launched themselves among the dogs to beat them away, afraid that the evidence of their prowess would be destroyed. John Peel had fulfilled his promise. Yet in his heart he wished otherwise. "Give me the tail," he said.

13

The *Great Michael* shuddered and listed as she changed direction. Meg walked carefully over the heaving deck and put her hand on the Fell Boy's shoulder. "We shall soon be stepping out onto a new land. You see in the distance? That horizon, that land is our new home."

"I feel sick," replied the Fell Boy, "something bad is out there. I feel sad."

"I know, my dear, I have watched you suffer. Your friend too is made low by your melancholy."

His small body buckled at the knees, and he slumped to the deck. Meg bent down and picked up the crumpled lad. "Quickly, get Captain Potter, clear his bunk. The child is sick. He has a fever!"

The Fell Boy was conscious, but the whites of his eyes were rolling, and he began to rant. "They've killed Cu'chulain! They've killed him! They're washing in his blood! They've murdered him, they've murdered him!"

Captain Potter appeared as if by magic, standing there with his arms crossed like a Turkish jinn. "Give the boy some hot water and whisky. I will have some fever powder made. Take him to my bunk."

Some of the crew stomped up the steps to the poop deck, where the Fell Boy was being carried to the Captain's cabin. Potter held out his hands. "Do not worry, lads and lasses, the boy has only taken a fever." He ushered the huddle back towards the rail. "We shall soon be at our new home. Free at last from our persecutors."

"Aye, 'tis been a long time coming, Cap'n," Renaldo said.

"Clear a space for me!" cried Captain Potter. The Giant Renaldo, with his huge shoulders, pushed the crew back gently, allowing Potter to move into the middle of them. "You have all served me well, and I note your concern for the boy. He shall be well again in a few days. I want you to know, after all that we've been through together, that I shall not desert you. When we reach the mainland, it will be each man for himself, but I shall not desert you." Potter looked into the distance. "Nay, perhaps we shall see each other again. But now it is time to return to the land and become farmers and fishermen. This is the way to avoid the unwanted attentions of the Empire. We have money, we have need and we have our freedom. Won for us by Cu'chulain." A great cheer went up. "We have had to abandon on the shores of Cumberland a host who have sailed with us. Our hunters, our animals and indeed our brave champion Cu'chulain."

"And above all, Mister Bibington," he said looking up to heaven, "I should have treated you as a better man." Then, looking down at his feet, he continued, "Not a night has gone by when I have not thought of our ship-mates who died in Whitehaven. And if it had not been for our hunters, we would not have made our fortune with the tiger wolf. We must remember them all. This is the coast where they found the beast. The hunters said it came to them. We return to this land now with thoughts of their loyalty to us." Looking at the veterans, he continued, "For this is a place where, though other folk think you ugly, the things that mark you different from other men shall be overlooked. And you shall be judged on your merits and the strength of your hearts."

The group gathering swayed gently, as the *Great Michael* heaved into the oncoming sea. Even as they listened intently to Captain Potter's final speech, some of the crew were making their way to vantage points near the aft of the vessel.

"It has taken us three months of hard sailing to reach these shores. Soon we shall be at anchor. Load all our supplies, ready for paradise island. We must sink the ship to the depths of Davey Jones, so there is no trace of her. We will take off her all that is useful." There were voices of dissent and then a gradual murmur of agreement.

"It must be so, it must be so," one of the veterans said. The Captain hung his head.

There was a brief silence before he finally said, "Right, return to your sta-tions. We sail for the final anchor point thirty-six degrees south by south-west."

Through the side of his mouth, he said to his acting First Officer, "These are exactly the same co-ordinates we used when we went ashore for the wolf creature. Oh, what a coming home."

Below in Potter's cabin, Meg tended to the Fell Boy, while his fox wait-ed in the shadows outside. He still rambled in his fever, "They've killed him, they've killed him. 'Tis a curse and I'll see him soon."

Meg applied cold compresses to his forehead and made sure that his head was supported on the bunk pillows, which she had made for the Captain. Above deck in the humid air, the crew heaved at ropes and took down sails, lest they might be seen by other ships. There was the sound of the spanking of feet on planks. Every so often, Meg could hear her husband bellowing commands, as the *Great Michael* punched her way through the swell. The door of the Captain's galley creaked open and Potter strode in, dripping salt water. He took Meg by the hand and pulled her towards him. Embracing her with a sense of urgency, he said, "My love, the long boats are being pre-pared for noon. Pack the best of our belongings. Money, jewels, firearms and food."

Meg smiled stoically at her husband and carried on. "The boy is sick. We should not be going now while he is recovering."

"We must go. There are sails on the horizon. I am afraid the *Great Michael* is about to become our betrayer. She must be scuttled."

Meg pushed herself away and strode through the cabin door. Then as loud as she could, she called, "Renaldo! Where is Renaldo? He must look to the boy!"

The Painted Lady answered Meg's call. "Renaldo is lowering the long ships. I shall fetch him."

As the crew gathered their belongings and any other items they could use in their new life, there was a sad methodic purpose to their work. Creaking ropes began to lower three longboats on to the turbulent Tasmanian sea. Renaldo picked up the boy and walked toward the last craft to be lowered. The fox followed closely behind. Standing by the *Great Michael's* wooden rails, the crew steadied the boats on their painters. Then the Captain emerged from his cabin with a huge axe. "Keep that last boat there, lads! I shall deal the death blow to the *Great Michael*. I shall break open the stop-cock and sink her." He slid down to the foc'sle and took a passage into the hold. Renaldo placed the boy gently into the final longboat, where several of the crew stood ready to lower it as soon the Captain returned. Meg continued to attend to the boy, while the fox stayed out of the way under one of the seats. But the *Great Michael* continued to circle about her anchor, riding the choppy swell.

"Make way together, men! Steer for the head point. Bear off, bowman!" the coxswain of the first boat shouted. "Pull together, pull with all your hearts!" The other coxswain repeated the order and two of the longboats pushed away from the *Great Michael*. They heaved across the tops of the waves with the tide following aft.

Now the *Great Michael* foundered. There was a great crack, as timbers cleaved apart and foam erupted into her insides. Her life ebbed away. Before the Captain knew it, water had reached his knees. Dropping the axe, he charged up the ship's ladder onto the poop deck. He lashed a rope to the handles of the wheel, so the ship would hold her course away from the escaping longboats. With the last of his crew still at their posts, he ran to the rails and slid down a rope into the final craft. On his signal, it was lowered into the sea. From their vessels the veterans kept their eyes fixed on those left aboard, keenly watching out for their welfare. They had fought hand to hand against Boney's Republican Guard, both sides too proud to give quarter, each veteran standing steadfastly next to his mate.

"Steady as she goes! Steady as she goes!" And then the final four crew men slid neatly down the ropes into the last longboat.

"Make for the coast, coxswain!" bellowed Potter over the sea. "Follow the others before we get dragged under by her death! Make way together, lads!" Oars rattled in the locks, gripping the water and speeding on the prow. No-one said a word. The Captain could not watch. Instead he turned and looked at the land that would be his new home. Meg, too, looked towards Van Diemen's Land, the land of Cu'chulain, the tiger wolf warrior. Before long the *Great Michael's* hull was sunk under the waves. All that could be seen were her masts protruding through the billows. A great air lock glugged its way to the surface from the belly of the ship. She was going down on her final voyage.

14

Matilda Dagobert had summoned the Member of Parliament of Whitehaven to meet her at Fenmore's Tea and Coffee House at the town's Central Gate. She had arrived at eleven clock sharp, helped on to the cobbles by her loyal manservant. Looking across the table at John Smith Wakefield, she said, "I understand there were some reprisals against your speech concerning the escaped slaves."

John Wakefield replied, "The current climate is for change, ma'am. There are many forces in Parliament that would gladly outlaw the practice of slavery."

Lady Dagobert sipped her small strong coffee. "The whole future of Whitehaven, both here and in the Indies, depends on our commitment to fighting the Abolitionists on all fronts and at whatever cost. Now kindly read me the escape of my slaves and their fate on the beaches of Morecambe Sands."

John Wakefield reached into his top coat and pulled out his spectacles. He arranged his papers in front of him "This is the report from the Member of Parliament for Morecambe Lancaster and Lonsdale, Bromley Atkinson," he said, and he began to read. "It has been brought to my attention that there was only one survivor of the terrible events on the shores of the furthermost reaches of my constituency, a certain negro by the name of Suniman. All other reported escapees were drowned in tragic circumstances after a particularly freak and fast tide. The bodies of all the fugitives were recovered and buried in sacred ground in the church cemetery at Bolton-le-Sands, the funerals and service paid for by the Quaker brethren residing nearby. The obsequies were well attended by senior members of the Abolitionist movement. I hold the Quaker brethren in the highest esteem. I understand that Suniman is making a full recovery and is being taught English and the Christian faith." John Wakefield finished reading, looked at Lady Dagobert and said, "My lady, are you all right? You appear a little pale."

Lady Dagobert replied, "I am afraid the affliction goes with the station, Mister Wakefield. I shall be fine after some more coffee."

Wakefield sat back in his chair and crossed his legs. "It is evident that Suniman has fallen in with quite an influential group. The Quaker brethren are not without significance, both in England and in the colonies, and I am told that he is being tutored to speak out against the practice of slavery."

"My God," Lady Dagobert said, "what will we and the Americas come to?

"

"It might be wise no longer to pursue the now redeemed slave, Suniman."

"You use the word 'redeemed', sir. May I remind you that he is mine."

"I beg to differ, my lady. Times have changed. The Abolitionists are not far from an overwhelming victory. And I have it on good authority that Suniman and his band were free men, African hunters merely working for the pirate Potter."

Lady Dagobert produced some smelling salts and began to sniff them. She then brought out a brightly painted fan and began to wave it at her cheeks. "I would like you to keep an eye on the progress of this Suniman. I have people to approach about the situation."

"With the greatest of respect, I would advise no further harassment of this particular man. I do not wish to offend my honourable friend and Member of Parliament for Morecambe and Lonsdale, who has a keen friendship with the Quaker movement."

Lady Dagobert looked like a petulant child. "I shall do what I will, sir. I always have." She rose from the table with difficulty but with dignity, turned her back on the politician and walked out of the coffee house.

TWO months later, Lady Dagobert held a Christmas ball to honour all those who had taken part in the hunt. What was left of the beast had been taken and stored in Keswick Museum for posterity. This included the creature's skull, its main skeleton and a portion of its hide. Although the death of the tiger wolf was seen to be a great victory for Lady Dagobert, the happy event was soured by a letter she received from an unknown location. It was from Captain Potter. There was no forwarding address. Shortly after the letter arrived, Lady Matilda Dagobert died in her sleep.

15
VAN DIEMEN'S LAND
1830-1832

Daniel Williamson, once the Fell Boy, was now a man with a son of his own, named David after his own murdered father. He too had shown a keen interest in animals, and now the family's reputation in Port Arthur of Van Diemen's Land was legendary. Any sick or ailing pet or beast was brought to them. If the owners could not pay, then the Williamson clan would barter for a cure.

Daniel narrowed his eyes and wrote in a new day and page of his diary.

Monday - I have heard my past master has been sighted with his fine lady wife on the reed banks near Hobart. It has been 20 years to this day since I last saw him. I am informed he is still in good spirits – when he does not consume them! And still the cock of all he surveys.

1400 hrs – cured the colic in McGrath's sheep; had to puncture stomach to let bad air escape, then stitch.

The farmers continue to kill the Tasmanian tiger. Never does God frown upon his children more than when they destroy this noble creature and my friend. I will try and help it all I can...

There was a loud bang at the door of the Williamson cabin. "Williamson! Yer services requested again down at the prison! Two of the horses have gone lame! Oh, and yer wife's begun labour!"

"Jesus Christ, Mary Mother of God! David, come with me to the jail. Yer mam needs us. She's in labour and we got work to do with the prison horses. C'mon now, put them down. They will look after themselves."

"Can I bring Petch? Can I bring him, Papa?"

Daniel's mind was taken back to the stocky insolent dwarf looking down at him in the rough and tumble of Whitehaven. "I think Petch is a good name for that vicious ugly polecat of yours," he said.

"But Papa, tell me again about the dwarfs and the tiger wolf and then I can name all me animals after them, after all them people in yer stories."

"C'mon, man!" snapped the turnkey. "C'mon, get them humpty dumpty legs in action! Did ye no hear me, yer wife is in labour, man!" He tightened his belt and put his warden's cap back on. "Ye can ride on the buggy. We have to get them horses right. I'll collect more prisoners from Hobart in the morn."

"Get up on the buggy, man. I will ride shotgun." Daniel and the turnkey climbed up and the warder lashed the horses fiercely with the reins. "Nay, steady on with them horses! Hold yer whip, man, ye skittered them! They just brought ye' eight miles." The horses snorted and whinnied, banging their hooves on the red earth below. Daniel looked round to see his son David tucked into the bottom of the buggy. He could smell the heavy sweat of the turnkey, who had pushed his horses along the cut through the Tasmanian jungle. The buggy rumbled on, watched by the angry eyes of the night prowlers and predators, the maulers and the great flesh-eating insects that devoured the land along with the humans.

The warder picked up a bottle that had fallen on the floor next to the saddle bags. "Take the reins, Williamson, I shall make this journey go faster." He uncorked the rum and swigged the bottle with deep glugs. Daniel smelt its distinct and seductive aroma. He flashed back again to the old country, where the melée of bloodshed, escaped animals, masked faces, violence and intolerance were all crunched in the jaws of a tiger wolf. "Man alive, ye're dead on yer feet! Ye nearly drove us into the tree!" Daniel tugged hard on the lead horse, turning the buggy back on to the track. "Here, give back the reins and get some of this down yer neck." The turnkey handed over the rum and Daniel also drank deep. Beneath the seat, young David pawed the turnkey's pistol, stroking the stock and gently fingering the trigger. The men's boots were just above him.

"I've been told by yer father-in-law that ye're coming on the drive!" The turnkey had to shout above the noise of the rumbling wheels, "and yer mongrel son and all!"

"Nay, nay, on account of veterinary business and even if the animals are not in need or want, I shall not bring me hand to aid and abet murderers and slavers."

"He will laugh into yer face again. Just because ye live with his daughter, do not think ye shall not fall foul of his wrath. Ye're on the payroll of the prison, Williamson. Like us all." The empty rum bottle was pitched out of the buggy. It smashed on the path.

"Aye, ye'd like to think so, ye crawling louse. Ye've been on the payroll longer than me and just maybe I've got other distractions."

As the turnkey threw his head back to laugh loudly, his cap rolled down his back and on to the boy. "Hold onto yer britches, man, we shall see who'll be spewing fire at the end of this night." The buggy bounced along the dirt track.

AS soon as the prison was visible, the drunken warder shouted for his mates. "C'mon, ye razzle dazzle boys. Come and get the quack and his son." The buggy came to a halt. The young lad vaulted over its side, clutching the pistol, which he hid in the back of his britches.

"Now, mister, show us the horses, so I can work me trade."

"Well, that is rum. That ye would rather tend to horses than visit yer wife in labour."

"Well, ain't that truth of it. But maybe ye should just take us over to see her."

The turnkey slapped him in the small of his back. "If ye take up with old Jenks here, he'll show you to the hospital."

Jenks avoided eye contact with everyone around him. "Aye, follow me. I'll take ye to the blood room. We've been punished by her birthing cries all through the night." The old turnkey looked up. "I hear the warden's expecting ye to take yer turn on the drive the morrow. 'Tis the big drive this time. We will be rid of all them savages. Them we don't despatch will be sent on to the mainland. D'you know them buggers broke in and stole some tools from the hardware store and then we found another so drunk in the creek that he would not have known if we had flayed him and given him a white skin."

"No good will come of it," Daniel said. "Ye think ye can just kill everything? Hunt it down and kill it? Or send it away? Just because ye got nothing between yer ears to understand anything other than eat, take, kill and burn."

"I got a notion ye're yella and I think that's come as a great pity to the old governor. Now stand back." Young David put his hand behind his back to touch the jag of the hard iron pistol, but he also felt his father's hand on his shoulder.

"Do ye know what I think? I think the whole gang of you are the offspring of Cain."

The second turnkey ushered the Williamsons into the blood room. Daniel's wife Mary, the daughter of the prison governor, was still in labour. She was circled by women, who made it hard for her husband to see her. "Come no closer. This is not pretty work and the baby's head is showing."

Daniel looked back at the door grimly, but stayed his ground. Instead, David moved outside, still fidgeting with the pistol.

"Fetch more hot water from the stove, Mister Williamson. Lend a hand instead of gawping. Ye shall soon have yer child."

Mary cried to God as she pushed.

"C'mon lass," said the midwife. "'Tis nearly over. One push more."

"I have it," cried another. "'Tis another lad."

Daniel moved to the fire and brought a copper pot of hot water over to where the women were. He handed it over gingerly. Now Mary was weeping with relief. Daniel tried to push his hand through the squad of women standing between him and his wife. He managed to touch her arm, before the truculent midwife said to him, "Away, man, away and do a man's work. Away, there is nought for ye here."

Mary piped up from the birthing table, "I am all right, Daniel, I am well. It was easier than David. Go and see my father. Tell him the news and make your peace with him, for God's sake. Make your peace with him. Please."

The baby took its first breath and cried long and loud. Daniel did not have to seek out his father-in-law, who was already stalking across the gravel towards the hospital. As Daniel opened the door, Governor Campbell was looking straight at him. "Ah, good. You come for your trade. And I have come for mine. I shall talk with you about the great drive and all our responsibilities."

Daniel quivered, his mouth drying so that he needed to swallow. "Mary says she is all right and we have another lad."

Campbell did not answer. Instead, he looked down on Daniel over the top of his beaked nose, unable to bend because of the starched white collar of his prison uniform. He was a stiff ibis of a man, devoid of all emotion and true moral conscience. Daniel was always intimidated in his presence. His son David was not.

"There have been several more incidents involving the natives. They have resisted all our attempts to subdue them and bring them into line with our Christian values. My situation here shall be compromised if I cannot subdue them. You, sir, are a simple man and, had I had the time to put a stop to your courtship with my daughter, you would have been on your way to Botany Bay, along with others of your kind who lack fortitude and moral fibre. What is worse, you are not merely a simple man, you are in fact a simple man bewildered by an unwise sense of false purpose. That is why tomorrow morning you shall join the other warders and settlers on the great drive. And we shall beat our way through Tasmania from coast to coast, flushing out these natives and putting an end to those who will not go. You and your son shall meet us in the morning at six of clock. You shall be issued with your carbine and your beater's paddles."

Daniel replied, "So 'tis done. But how is it? What about the lame horses?"

Campbell looked up into the air, "Oh, that was an erroneous report. All the horse teams for the prison cages are quite healthy."

Daniel's leg twitched uncontrollably, the iron tip of his toe clicking on the timber step at the door. He wondered how this man's religion, his perception of the world, could be so different to his own. But as the governor turned to walk away, Daniel saw not a man, but a nightmare of past torment. He put his hand onto his son's shoulder and found that the boy had changed his position, an arm outstretched and pointing a pistol in the direction of his grandfather, the governor. The insects were chirping and clicking their dirges all around. Daniel closed his palm around the weapon, breaking the boy's grip gently and with understanding.

16

The next morning, the turnkeys were breaking out government issue rifles for the farmer settlers who had come to annihilate and deport the natives. One carbine was allotted to every half dozen men.

"So, number six, make sure ye can use it," the turnkey said, as he handed a gun to Daniel. "Pleased ye could join us today and as ye can see, we have captured some Abbos who attacked Farmer Selkirk with spears through the night." The turnkey pointed at the red-haired Tasmanian Aborigines natives manacled around the roots of a gum tree. "Perhaps we should have killed them. Anyhow, they are being shipped to the islands in Bass Strait. Or who is safe here?"

Daniel had taken charge of the pistol. It was now stashed away in his trouser pocket.

"You lads can start beating on the line, starting at the prison fence. Look lively." The turnkey walked back toward his mates, who stood drinking mugs of strong coffee to sober them up. As Daniel and his son moved to their positions in the line, he saw his distant neighbours, awkward among the sudden crowd. Things were not easy any more, so his fellow beaters were saying. Then a weary Jacobite from the old country piped up that Van Diemen's Land was under martial law. "Can I not be free? Can I not be free from their whip?"

The gun sounded from the prison walls and the men moved forward, slapping the bush and reeds with their heavy sticks and swinging the bull-roarers. The sun was rising to meet them, the scorch of its heat causing the beaters to cup their hands over their eyes. The line moved deeper into the bush. Sometimes an animal would be made to bolt with surprise, and then rounds of shot would be fired down the ways. Campbell watched from his tower. From there, he could see for miles over his land.

The first casualty now fell victim to the line. A white settler blasted a native through his back as he would a kangaroo. The men broke loose to come and look at the corpse lying in the bushes. Daniel averted his eyes and died once more within. Another man from the line moved up to Daniel. "Ye see how easy it is. Do ye think ye can do that? Now get."

Daniel looked at him with funeral eyes. "That man had nay no chance. Ye did not even try and restrain him. Ye just pistolled him like vermin."

"Yer turn to try next, boy," the line executioner sneered. Daniel looked down at his son, but he was fixed on the dead Aboriginal, stretched out on the ground in front of him.

"C'mon, c'mon!" cried another of the turnkeys. "Let's move on! By the time we come back this evening, he will have turned white." The line moved on and the men worked up a sweat, beating the forest and bashing cans together to make a din. Once more, further down the line, another shot was fired, but it was not a native, just an animal that they had winged or killed. All the time the men bantered between one another, when they weren't panting for breath in the humidity. Sometimes bright parakeets and finches took to the air, their wings fluttering in panic as the men moved forwards across the island. The settlers proclaimed their stake on the land, each encouraging the next in their quarter of the line to be the next to be ready to kill. Now the natives were streaking ahead of the drive, the men and women heading north away from the white snake with red necks that slid after them.

At breakfast time, the Port Arthur men stopped and piled up their trophies. They had a tally, while they waited on the tucker wagons. Several adult kangaroos were laid out in the grass. And arranged as a head-dress lay koala bears and other small mammals. But the dead native had been dumped. When the wagons arrived, they pulled up in front of the shot animals and began to serve coffee, bread and bacon. Daniel perspired in the heat, while his son shivered and was ashen in the face.

Before the tucker carts had gone, news of yet more native kills ran down the line. Two more, nay three, and a woman. The men smiled at one another. They were feeling good about working together. Half an hour later, they came upon a small family crying into the ground. They were pulling at each other's hair and tried to bury their faces in the scrub. The settlers were soon upon them. Two of the fiercer-looking men were bludgeoned about the head, whilst the younger men and women and children were rounded in a huddle and marched to the nearest cut to wait for the penitentiary wagons for deportation. Many of the men of the line booed those first on the scene with cries of, "Take a scalp! Shoot them!" And there was much laughter.

Behind Daniel, two turnkeys were following his steps as he advanced with the line. "Check yer weapon, Williamson. Make sure ye not wasting ammunition. Ye killed nothing." They pulled the gun out of his hands. "Ye better do something before twelve noon, or we have to give it to somebody with guts." Daniel held out his hands to take back the weapon and said nothing, "and as for you, young fellow, have no fear, yer father will make a score yet." And then the warder patted the boy's head.

Turning to his son and looking down through red eyes, Daniel said under his breath, "Yes, I shall make a score before this day is finished."

Another hour passed. More natives had been dragged out of the undergrowth by the Port Arthur men. Sometimes the women were manhandled and treated lewdly. Sometimes they were raped. The line moved over the blood of the victims and the animals. And still Daniel had not killed. Settlers on either side of him moved away, as their fob watches ticked towards twelve clock. Following up the rear, the Port Arthur prison wagons were crammed to capacity with their sorry charges. The settlers did not have it all their own way. A white-bearded farmer was hit by a short dart thrown from the bush. Rarely did these men die. The stabs served only to drive them on to further levels of sadistic frenzy against the natural inhabitants. The torture and hard labour ladled on the white prison inmates paled beside what the natives were suffering.

At twelve clock, the turnkeys returned to find Daniel sitting on a rock looking at his boots, his rifle propped up against a tree. One warder took up Daniel's rifle, while the other guard covered Daniel with his own piece. Daniel remained silent. The others in the line moved further away into the scrub, shaking their heads with embarrassment. And then nature struck back. Rearing up from the greenery, a tiger wolf set of huge jaws leapt on to the turnkey who was covering Daniel. Its ivory white teeth closed on the man's neck, tearing his windpipe. He was dead before he hit the ground.

Daniel fell back from the rock. His son David moved next to him, the long tail of the wolf beast brushing past both of them. "It's come back!" they both cried. Turning about, the beast savaged Daniel's neighbour Peter McGrath. It did not kill him, but it tore some muscles from his chest and bolted back into the bush. In the distance men fired useless shots, but the creature had gone. Panic seized the Port Arthur line. The hunters dropped to their knees and bellies in the undergrowth to seek cover. This cowardice gave Daniel time to consider his next move.

Turning to his son he said, "Ye must make get away. Go back to our cabin and look under the floorboards, under the potions cabinet. Ye will find some things and how to get to a man who can help ye. God willing, he is still living. Go now, while the line is confused. 'Twill be yer only chance." The boy hugged his father and gripped his shirt tightly. Daniel had to unpeel his fingers slowly and push the boy away for his own good. Then with tears in his eyes, David slunk away from the holocaust into the green wilderness. In Daniel's mind, there was one man to blame, as the white settlers bound him in chains. But his heart cried out at the victory of the lone striped beast. When news of the next tally came rolling down the line from one settler to his neighbour, he heard that many tiger wolves had been shot. The government bounty had been set at ten shillings per head.

Shortly after noon, Campbell arrived on the scene to see what progress his men had made and to congratulate them on their work against the natives. He emerged from a covered prison wagon, drinking local papaya juice from a crystal glass. Daniel waited in shackles. Before the governor's long boots touched the dirt, a great cheer went up from the line. And then the settlers brought out the wounded tiger wolf, setting it carefully on a flat rock. The men looked proud, but Daniel crawled towards the creature in its chains, to the amusement of his father-in-law.

"It seems, my poor Daniel, that you are a man who cannot take the opportunity of hope." He sauntered closer, yet kept his distance from the pair. Daniel felt the dying breaths of the panting beast on his body. The great head lolling to one side hung over the rock. Although its eyes were glazed, there were still flashes of golden life. He remembered back to when he freed Cu'chulain in those sorry years so long ago. And then the red mist came back with a stab of ice in his soul against the heat of the bush. Daniel rose to his feet, his chains clinking against the rock where the tiger wolf lay.

Campbell smiled, "Another one of your loves, so they tell me. How shall we ever replace the good warder who was killed by its kind? I think a couple of years hard labour at Hobart will settle your hash." Daniel felt for the pistol, his thin wrists pushing through the iron manacle deep into his pocket. The butt went to his hand. Campbell moved forward. Some of the men nodded and smiled, trying to catch the governor's attention. "We have had a good morning. We have captured at least a hundred savages, who shall shortly be on their way to Bass Strait. Unluckily, several have been killed. We have a few tiger wolves and a big bag of kangaroos and the like. And now I have you, shown up for what you are."

The men nearest to the prison governor were snickering, as they moved to drag the dead turnkey out of the mud. Now through his red mist, Daniel could see Campbell's great white head as a target. As the haze drew away from his eyes, Daniel pulled out the pistol and pointed it coolly at Campbell's head. The governor's face remained blank. He could not comprehend what was happening. He had no concept of his own death. The settlers were silent. None of them had expected this. Campbell's mouth opened to utter the word, "Stupid." Carefully, Daniel pulled the trigger, his aim true. There was a snap from the gun and a dull thud. A small red hole appeared above the governor's nose. Daniel saw the white skin crinkle around its perimeter, the word, "Stupid" fixed in the death gape. And then Campbell fell backwards to his grave.

17

"Williamson, here's your slop!" Rotten gruel was pushed under the door at seven-thirty in the morning. Daniel took hold of the pewter bowl and drank the soft muck. This would be the day of the visits. He had been confined now for three months in Port Arthur Prison, his trial set for the 31 August, 1832. The turnkeys were no longer taking orders from the dead man who had persecuted him. He was a goner and things had changed. And the law had to take its turn.

At nine-thirty, Daniel's door was opened and his lawyer sidled inside the cell. He offered his hand to Daniel, who shook it with both hands.

"It appears fortune favours the brave. And for you, Daniel Williamson, condemned to death at the gallows, there is an ironic situation. I believe you shall meet your benefactor within the week. I am under his instruction to defend you from having your neck stretched."

Daniel sagged in his grey prison suit, while the lawyer moved closer to him.

"You shall have a visit from your benefactor. He draws near. But in the meantime, as your representative in the Crown versus Daniel Williamson, I require you to report the details of your experiences and adventures and why you killed your father-in-law. It seems that he had many enemies, and you have many friends. It must be said that your case has caused considerable interest, even with our monarch and their royal highnesses. Politicians too, whatever they are worth."

Daniel looked at the lawyer. "My son David has possession of my diaries, Mister Sinclair. These will furnish ye with all ye need to know. What news of him? How has he fared? Where has he gone? And what of my wife Mary?"

Sinclair fingered his goatee beard, "All shall be revealed shortly, sir, the whole story told. It is rather more complicated with your wife, as she now wants to sever all connections with you in terms of law. I regret to inform you that she wants to divorce you."

Daniel was not surprised. He scraped his fingers along the rough wooden table of his cell. Outside the heavy iron prison door, the turnkeys had changed their views again. "Well, ye've got to admire him. He's got balls all right. Everybody got him marked for yella and then suddenly he brings out his cannon and shoots God. The murder trial is one week hence. Everybody's sure he'll swing. 'Twill be the greatest kick yer toes the Port has ever seen."

Sinclair banged on the cell door and the warders came. As the lawyer put on his hat, Daniel said, "What news of the drive? What did they do?"

"Well, the issue remains. Many famous people have spoken against the drive. Even Charles Darwin has condemned the atrocities as being crimes against humanity, brutal beyond belief. Count Strzelecki is shocked to the core. Now all Europe must be aware of this barbarous method of ridding our land of its natives."

"And what of the tiger wolf?"

"A bounty has been fixed. The settlers are frightened to death. For they say it steals their sheep and has the audacity to attack humans. They say it watches them, staring them out, studying them. Waiting all the time. Waiting."

Daniel held his hand to his forehead. "They can't bear its spirit. It moves mysterious with our great Creator. They do not believe animals have spirits. They think everything is dead as they are."

Sinclair stood up and looked down at Daniel. "Yes, it is indeed a strange beast. I must confess I shall have a hard time acquainting myself with this curious country. Good day." The cell door was pulled shut. Daniel was on his own again.

LATER that day Daniel was woken by the rattle of keys. He sat and waited. Governor Pritchett walked into the cell. Daniel lifted his legs off the bed and stood. "Sit down, Williamson. You do not have to stand on my account." The turnkeys were hovering around the door. "Dismiss. Come back in five minutes." The door slammed shut behind him. "Now then, Williamson, you see I can face you man to man, even though you blasted the head off the man before me." Pritchett looked Daniel in the eye.

Daniel was surprised at this unexpected visit. Nervous, he began to talk at the floorboards. "Is Mister Sinclair coming again? When will he be here?"

"We have received a rather handsome donation from your benefactor. He is waiting to see you with his good lady wife. Let us hope that this man's interest in your redemption shall save you from the gallows."

Pritchett pulled a rickety chair from under the table and sat down. "I wanted to see you for myself. I wanted to face the man who so coldly killed my predecessor." His tone was questioning. "I call him my predecessor, and I believe he was your reluctant father-in-law."

Daniel looked up from the floor. "Well, I did not choose him. I was with his kin. His daughter was my wife. She was with child before we had time to marry. He hated me. That was not new. He hated all - the animals, the people, the settlers, and himself he hated too."

Pritchett listened intently. "Continue," he said.

Daniel poured forth, "Mary and I were only young when we met. I had got the ability for the animals. I mended them. I got them better. I repaired them. Sometimes I grew them when their mother died. I loved the horses, the fine noble horses. Always pulling the logs from forest or taking prisoners in carts, never complaining. And the dogs - seems they can take no end of boot from settlers. Always lashing out and kicking them and still they come back and be their friend. When ye woke in the morning, there were birds at yer window with seed in their bill. While settlers pulled the plough, I was birthing lambs from their mothers. For such, Campbell hated me, but still he brought me in to look after the animals." Daniel was speaking out at last. "A time past, when I came to this land from the old country, I brought with me a young fox. It stopped with me for some time and then went off on its own. It met another other of its kind, a red one just like him. I reckoned that it was only one, but I was wrong, guv'ner. For there were more. Sometimes it came back to the cabin, peeking behind the plants, but it had its own life, so I let it be."

Pritchett was now looking at the floor. "And what of the drive, the infamous drive?"

"There was no worse thing for me than being part of that drive. Listen, guv'ner, ye can hear shots miles north. Ye can still hear shots. Do ye think it's something God wants, this? All this killing? When will it stop?"

Pritchett lifted his eyes, "Well, I am under orders from the government. Although I must say, I detest these foul plans. And I am not alone in my convictions. The murder of Governor Campbell has sent shockwaves all through the mainland and in Europe. Who knows what will happen? Your case, although it be a small part of the great Tasmanian drive, has been taken up by the Abolitionists, and I am told that a group proclaiming to do the will of God has pledged to sail from England. Like others of their kind, they are highly connected, their families intertwined with the Quaker movement."

The turnkey banged on the cell door, "Five minutes, guv'ner. Yer guests are back, sir."

"It is time to go." Pritchett looked down at Daniel, "Here's something from your visitors to help your salvation. Now that you are notorious." And he plopped a leather Bible on the table and walked out. After the cell door slammed shut, the prisoner heard the footsteps of the governor echoing down the avenue of cells. And yet again, Daniel felt what it was like to be a caged bird or animal. He looked through the rusty bars of his tiny cell to a green wall of forest. He had contemplated a break out, yet he believed that some weird action of fate was working in his favour. He did not want to run forever like the beast, turning with ferocity on his tormentors.

Leaning forward on the creaky chair, he picked up the Bible and opened it at a leather marker. He began to read from the Book of Daniel, Chapter Six, verse twenty-seven. "He delivers and rescues, he works signs and wonders in heaven and on earth, he who has saved Daniel from the powers of the lions."

He turned to the beginning of the Bible. Written in ink on the flyleaf was a familiar hand. It said: "To Daniel Williamson, whom we have never forgotten. Mr & Mrs Potter, the year of our Lord, 1832."

A rush of excitement ran through Daniel. More footsteps sounded outside the cell. These were followed by the cries and shouts of prisoners, who banged their iron doors and rattled their pewter spoons. There were lewd screams and curses. Pritchett glared at the turnkeys, who were soon rattling keys in the cell doors of the shouters. They slugged the inmates with their wooden truncheons, stopping the flow of filth from their mouths. Then the door of Daniel's cell was opened. Standing there with the governor were a man and woman he had not seen for twenty years. They entered casually, as if they had only left him for a week.

"Ah, Daniel," Potter said, "it breaks my heart to see you in this predicament. But let us throw ourselves on the mercy of the Lord, who forgives all our sins."

Pritchett nodded his solemn agreement and took a step back. "If you need anything at all, Mister Potter - tea for your good lady wife - there will be warders stationed for the duration of your visit." But before he departed, he said with an odd smile, "Perhaps you will join me later in the chapel to pray for the souls of the condemned?"

The door was closed, fastening them all in the cell. Daniel could not speak. He sat flinching at the gunshots from the hill above the great green bank outside his cell. Mr and Mrs Potter were dressed in black and grey, their faces lined by the sun and their labours. Daniel moved to meet them as a child wanting an embrace, but the man extended his hand to shake. The old sea captain kept back the great emotion of his life behind a hard bleak face. Meg grasped his arm, as always by his side. The old sailor's thatch had now thinned and was now white.

"Pay no heed to our sombre aspect," Potter said. "We are the same people you once knew." He winked at Daniel.

Meg smiled peacefully, "We are in disguise, but even so, we have read the good book. And we have both made our peace with our eternal father."

Daniel motioned towards Meg, taking hold of her hand and kissing her cheek. Her past beauty had retreated, but now, what was within?

Daniel took a step back and said, "I am not afeared to swing."

"Tis the way of things," the Captain said, "Tis just the way of the world."

Meg straightened, "But look to the good at Hobart. Look at the support and reform barracks we have built with the money."

Daniel's jaw tensed, "What of my son, young David? What of my diaries and my gelt? Is my son safe?"

Meg moved forward, "They cannot chase him. He has done no crime. I have put him to work at the vet farm in the estate of the reformed prisoners."

Daniel's jaw loosened. Captain Potter fingered his throat. "You shall not swing, for I have offered a large donation to the Port Arthur Penitentiary. They need money. And this governor is sympathetic, for he walks the Quaker way." Potter's eyes twinkled with mischief. "You see, our fates are entwined. It was meant to be that I should save you from yourself. You did not fit into the scheme of things, Daniel Williamson."

Daniel looked at the ceiling, "And what with those killing beasts who call themselves men?"

"I am afraid," Potter continued, "the drive continues and is moving north across the island. It moves with a rage inspired by evil. And I thought we had got away from that kind."

Meg put her hand on his shoulder, "Come, my love. You have saved us all. Now we must prepare our way by saving Daniel."

18

Next day, Daniel was taken out of his cell for the first time in two months and marched to be exercised in a small covered yard. Here he clumped with the other convicts around an iron-hard warder. He was now among the favoured men of the Port Arthur Penitentiary. Most of the men dragged chains with a heavy iron ball attached. Daniel had manacles on his ankles that allowed him to shuffle through the sand. A preacher walked in through the yard entrance, followed closely by the new prison governor. The prisoners, who tramped a circle in the sand, were broken up by the turnkey and pushed into ranks as if they were soldiers.

An old lag mumbled from the side of his mouth, "How didst thou find thy way here amongst us reprieved men, Daniel Williamson? For thou art a murderer." His words were cut short by the warder's staff, which thwacked the back of his neck, stunning him.

Daniel hit back, "I am no murderer. and the world will be a better place without that bad man." The staff was turned on Daniel. He flinched as it cracked his collar bone.

"Silence, sinners," the turnkey said, "the preacher speaks." The men bent their heads in obedience.

"All ye who have strayed from the narrow path," the preacher said, "repent and be forgiven. Repent and save your souls. You are the broken men and the black sheep of the flock. For your own sake, make restitution and bring the Good Shepherd into your life. There is a way to return to the straight and narrow path of the Lord, which beginneth with the purity of hard labour. Cast your eyes upon the rocks that weep, for these shall be your forty days in the wilderness, as you break them with your hammers."

Some of the prisoners held their shackles to their chests and looked to the sky, shouting, "Praise be the Lord!" Their faces lit with a new experience, or the pretence of one.

The preacher continued, "So if you would kindly join me in the Lord's prayer. And we say together, Our father who art in Heaven..." All the prisoners joined in, chuntering along with their beards moving to the rhythm of the prayer. "...Hallowed be thy name. Thy kingdom come. Thy will be done on earth as it is in Heaven. Give us this day our daily bread, and forgive us our trespasses, as we forgive those who trespass against us. And lead us not into temptation, but deliver us from evil. For thine is the kingdom, the power and the glory. For ever and ever. Amen."

Then Governor Pritchett stepped forward, holding a Bible, "Reading from Daniel Four, verses ten to sixteen. And behold a tree in the midst of the earth, and the height thereof was great. The tree grew, and was strong, and the height thereof reached unto heaven, and the sight thereof to the end of all the earth. The leaves thereof were fair, and the fruit thereof much, and in it was meat for all. The beasts of the field had shadow under it, and the fowls of the heaven dwelt in the boughs thereof, and all flesh was fed of it. I saw in the visions of my head upon my bed, and, behold, a watcher and an holy one came down from heaven. He cried aloud, and said thus, hew down the tree, and cut off his branches, shake off his leaves, and scatter his fruit. Let the beasts get away from under it, and the fowls from his branches. Nevertheless, leave the stump of his roots in the earth, even with a band of iron and brass, in the tender grass of the field; and let it be wet with the dew of heaven, and let his portion be with the beasts in the grass of the earth. Let his heart be changed from man's, and let a beast's heart be given unto him."

Daniel straightened his hunched shoulders, as he recognised the governor's message. The other convicts' irons and chains clanged gently as their boots scuffed the sand. The governor closed the Bible and looked to the preacher. The sinners filed out through the entrance to the covered yard, where they were met by more armed officers.

The man with the short staff put it across Daniel's chest, barring his way, so that he stopped in his tracks. "Ye have work with the animals, follow me." A convict to the rear of the trundling line scowled back through rimmed eyes, but Daniel did not care, for he was pushed into the back of an open buggy. He was driven to the end farms, where he was pulled out of the carriage on to his knees. When he looked up, he saw a pen full of hogs. They snorted and grunted at their troughs, their ears jiggling about their bristled heads.

"Ye can start by feeding the rest of the slops to the porkers. We'll be watching ye with a rifle. So don't be thinking ye'll be getting off easy like." Daniel pushed himself up and entered the pen, closing the gate behind him. "Might be a harder death than swinging, Daniel lad, being gutted by one of them big sows."

But Daniel was unafraid, as he went about his task, while the warders wagered how long it would take before he was gored by a hog's tusk. He fetched and carried and tipped the vile food slops into the troughs. The hogs brushed against him, their rough sides pricking his flesh. He never lashed out or kicked the hogs, but was gentle with them, nudging his way through their mass with his knees. When his task was done, he bent low and began to shovel their shit. And yet still the great sows with their suckling piglets ignored him. The big tusks hooking out from the boars' jaws did not pierce him. All around the dust rose high into the air, as trotters kicked the earth. Day after day he laboured in the hog pens. At night he was taken under armed guard for his meal and bedded down in the stables with the horses.

Soon Daniel was set to work in more fulfilling ways. He laboured twelve and fourteen hours a day repairing the bodies of the prison animals. He broke in horses in his gentle and knowing way. He calmed down mares for the blacksmith and helped to bring the sheepdog pups into the world. Never was a man worked so hard at the task he loved most. All the time he did not speak, but he dreamt of a time when men and beasts and the land might be one. And each day of his toil on the farm brought him closer to the sentence of his death.

Finally, Daniel Williamson was ordered for trial on the 14 May, 1832. By now eighteen months of imprisonment had turned the warders' derision to a grudging respect. They too brought him their animals to tend, under the watchful eye of the new prison governor, who often charged them for Daniel's compassion.

19

The morning of his trial Daniel was taken in irons to have his head shaved and deloused. Once dressed in prison uniform with arrows and POM emblazoned across the back, he was made to stand in chains in the back of an open buggy, as in a tumbrel being taken to the guillotine. Scores of settlers lined the roadside to see the man who had shot the vicious old governor, but cared for the animals. They did not scream at him. They averted their eyes as he rumbled past to the Port Arthur courthouse.

When Daniel was escorted into the courtroom, it was packed. Rich and poor, men of mixed caste, sailors and sea captains, mothers and old women, all came to look on the face of the man who shot Campbell. The judge sat under his wig, while to his left a sombre jury waited for the trial to begin. In the crowd to the back were Mr and Mrs Potter with other Quaker brethren. They sat with hands clasped in meditation and prayer. After the opening statements had been made, the prosecuting counsel called Daniel to the stand for questioning. "You are Daniel Williamson of Wolf Cabin, Deep Cutting, Port Arthur?"

"I am, sir."

"Are you an educated man, Daniel Williamson?"

"I am not, sir."

"But you do have a particular way of mending animals, do you not?"

"A gift from God, sir."

There were mutters from the stalls. Then a lady stood up and shouted, "He mended my Clydesdale! It would have gone to the knackers if not for him and he saved us!"

The judge banged his gavel. "Silence! This is not a music hall!" The crowd went quiet and the prosecution for the Crown against Daniel Williamson continued. Witnesses were called forward who lied about Daniel's character and nature. They said he was a coward. He would not help rid the land of the vicious natives and evil beasts that lurked in the bush. But Daniel's defence was clever. Those who testified were simple farmers and settlers, ridden with guilt about the part they had played in the great drive. Sinclair used the backlash against Daniel's accusers.

Prison Officer Adams was called to the dock. The judge banged his gavel once again, crying, "Order in court!" The turnkey took the stand and swore his oath.

"You have a particularly difficult profession, do you not, Mister Adams?"

counsel asked.

"Aye, sir, I do."

"And you were one of the men who witnessed at first hand the death of your prison governor, is that correct?"

The heavy guard answered, "Aye, sir, I saw Daniel Williamson pull out a pistol and shoot the guv'ner between the eyes. He fell down dead as a doornail. It weren't regular. Daniel? He wouldn't kill nothing or nobody. It were a joke."

"That being so, Mister Adams, where did the revolver come from? How did Daniel Williamson come to possess it?"

"It was the personal pistol of Officer Atholl Macintyre, sent to collect Daniel Williamson and his son for vet'inary services on the order of Guv'ner Campbell."

The prosecution thought it wise to stop there and dismissed the witness.

Sinclair took the floor, "Call Atholl Macintyre."

Like his colleague, Macintyre looked uneasy. Sinclair moved forward. "What, Officer Macintyre, were your orders on the night you fetched Daniel and his son to come to the prison?"

"Well, sir, I confess that night I took the opportunity, on account of the long journey to Daniel's, to take a little refreshment. Ye know, to make the journey go faster. Guv'ner Campbell told me to bring Daniel to the prison at any cost. He set a plan, as there were sick horses. He knew Daniel would come for them and his wife Mary was having little Matty."

"And what about your prison issue pistol, Officer Macintyre?"

"Not a prison pistol, but my own, sir. I'd been using it to keep away them tiger wolves. The bush is thick with them."

"So what make was your pistol?"

"Two barrel, sir, not one."

"What happened then?"

"Well, by that time, me and vet'nary were drinking down and some. There's no way Daniel would think to steal it and I seen him, as he was sat next to me. Nah, if ye ask me, that nipper of his, David, nicked the gun."

A burble of laughter rose up from the gallery.

"That will be all," Sinclair said.

MURDER was beginning to look more like manslaughter. And by the time the defence had begun four days into the trial, more and more people in dark clothes filled the stalls. Glances met across the courtroom with those of the jury. Counsel was becoming perplexed at the growing presence of reformers and Quakers. The witnesses who came forward testified to the cruel and barbarous nature of Daniel's father-in-law.

Then a strange witness from the past was summoned to the stand. "I call Suniman Fry of the Quaker Meeting House, Lancaster, England," Sinclair said. A large shadow fell upon the outer wall of the courthouse. The bailiff opened the courtroom door and Suniman stepped within. He too was dressed in black and carried a brimmed hat by his side. Twenty-one years amongst the Quaker brethren of north west England had turned the Ethopian hunter into a spokesman of the Lord. Solomon strode in for the judgement. Mr and Mrs Potter could not hide their shock on seeing the face of the man who had captured the tiger wolf so long ago. The sight was more than religion and sobriety could stand. Potter brought out a hip flask and swigged from it, popping it back into his inner coat pocket. Meg shifted uncomfortably and looked away, her cheeks flushed.

The man of God turned directly to the gallery and looked long and deep at the face of the Captain, who had deserted him on the desperate shores of England. His gaze then fell on the tiny figure of Petch. Time had been good to this child of the Scarlet Circus. But it had been even kinder to Suniman, as he passed the years in contemplation and study. The voice boomed again. "Suniman Fry, please take the stand." Sinclair then asked for his details, after he had sworn his oath.

"I am Suniman Fry, formerly of the continent known as Africa, the eastern Horn. I have lived in service to my keepers, the Quaker brethren of Lancaster, for twenty-two years. I am a free man and now an active member of the Agency Committee. Our purpose is to put an end to slavery. I myself have never been a slave. But I have been treated as one."

Sinclair interrupted momentarily, "We have heard of the Lancaster brethren's work with the Abolition movement and how they choose to lead by example. You are not the only man or woman that they have rehabilitated in the name of God. Is that not correct?"

"No, sir, it is our duty to save those that mankind has chosen to enslave. And our duty to enlighten with the word of God those who have been made low by man."

"Why have you come to Van Diemen's Land, Mr Fry?"

"Because it is my calling. We minister and enlighten where there is darkness. And the victims of the evil drive have been in our prayers almost continuously for the past eighteen months. I myself was the sole survivor, where my brother hunters and two dozen slaves were marched from Whitehaven, only to be drowned on the shores of Morecambe Bay. Had it not been for the ministry of the Quaker brethren upon my soul and..." Suniman paused, "...and had not all my fellow hunters been drowned on these same shores, then we would all most certainly have been pressed into a life of misery and cruelty."

Counsel stood forward, "Objection, my lord. This is irrelevant."

"Objection overruled. I am interested in Mr Fry's testimony."

The Potters and Petch shifted on their hard wooden bench, as Suniman spoke of his fate. The Captain sneaked another swig from his snug hip flask. Daniel stared into another world. He was remembering the mighty hunter with bull-hide shield and stabbing spear. The man, who had caught the tiger wolf, had returned to free its liberator.

"Please continue, Mr Fry," Sinclair said.

"I have brought evidence and individual testimonies as to the barbarous and evil nature of the former governor of Port Arthur Penitentiary, James Campbell. This man was appointed, not because he was a good prison governor, but because of his experience as a slaver in the Indies and the Americas." A great sigh rose in court. "Campbell has been linked with tyranny against our brothers and sisters of the Black Continent for two generations, and his father before him. You may also be aware that, as the government of the Mother Country is compensating families who desist in this evil trade, they are also appointing these same brutes into positions of authority all over the Empire. And I declare that this is the truth of the matter in the late Governor Campbell's appointment."

The judge conferred with the clerk before his seat and banged his gavel once again. "Court adjourned," he declared. "Cross-examination of the defence shall begin tomorrow."

There was a hubbub in the courtroom. The doors burst open. The gallery spilled into the crowd on the steps outside. There was a scream as a juror was pushed into a man with a hollow in the side of his face, one of the war veterans from Captain Potter's crew, ancient now, but free. Further down the steps, a young lady was carried to safety like a weightless puppet by the Great Renaldo, still an oak even beyond his prime.

THE nest morning, the cross-examination of the defence did not go well. Suniman ran rings round the prosecution. But counsel had a surprise witness who would surely guarantee a guilty verdict on the charge of murder.

"Call Mary Williamson, formerly the wife of the accused."

There was a gasp from the gallery. Daniel hung his head, closing his heavy eyelids and thinking back to better times. Mary was helped into the dock by the bailiff. She stared remorsefully at Daniel, as she took her oath.

The prosecution put the question, "You were, were you not, formerly the wife of the accused, Daniel Williamson?"

"Yes, sir, I was, and still am. We are not yet divorced."

"Could you describe to the court the relationship between the accused, Daniel Williamson, and the deceased, Governor Campbell?"

Mary watched the clock on the far wall. "It was my fault, I am sure. Because I chose a man so different from my father. He detested what he considered to be weakness in Daniel's character." She paused, thinking over her next sentence. "Weakness that I now know without a doubt was strength."

There was a murmur of confusion from the gallery, and counsel looked dumbstruck. He tipped his wig and carried on, "But the case remains that this man, your former husband, shot and killed your father."

Mary gripped the moulded woodwork of the stand, "If Daniel had not killed my father, then my father would most certainly have killed him." Counsel's eyes widened in horror, but before he had a chance to interrupt, Mary continued, "My father's hatred now seems truly diabolical. For Daniel was an innocent, content with his profession as a veterinary doctor. All my father ever did was destroy, and often kill through the work of others."

The Queen's Counsel readjusted his wig again, "That will be all, Mrs Campbell. Sorry, Mrs Williamson."

As the bailiff pulled her roughly from the witness box, she shouted across the courtroom, "The truth will out, Daniel. The truth will out!" All counsel could say was, "The poor woman is clearly deranged."

THE prosecution's summing up was eloquent. "We are dealing here with facts. Despite all you have heard about the current state of politics in the slave trade, there are no legal slaves in Van Diemen's Land. This case has nothing whatsoever to do with slavery. The shot fired against Governor Campbell was premeditated, a heinous act of murder, for which there can only be one sentence. That is that Daniel Williamson shall be hung by the neck until he is dead, in accordance with the laws of the land. Any other verdict would be an open act of rebellion against the Crown."

The jury looked on solemnly, burdened by the responsibility of judgement. But they seemed to have joined the people in the gallery, who appeared to be more part of a silent prayer meeting than an audience. They were only two hours out of the courtroom when they returned and the judge instructed them to announce their decision. The foreman stood impassively next to his fellows. The judge looked down and said, "Have you reached a verdict?"

"Yes, my Lord."

"Do you find the accused, Daniel Williamson, guilty of murder as charged?"

"Not guilty."

A great cheer sounded. "Silence!" cried the judge, his words cutting through the stale air. "Do you find the witness guilty of the lesser charge of manslaughter?"

"Guilty, my lord." Joy gave way to silence. The judge had to pronounce sentence. He touched the black death cap that would have been placed on Daniel's head, if he had been found guilty of murder.

"Daniel Williamson, you are a fortunate man to have escaped pain of death. In the current political climate, you have drawn many supporters to your cause. Nevertheless, it is my duty to issue you with your sentence. You shall be sentenced to life imprisonment, which is the maximum sentence according to English law. For the rest of your life, you are sentenced to hard labour in the Port Arthur Penitentiary. The nature of your labours shall be the duty of the governor to determine. He shall be your keeper from now until your death. Have you anything to say for yourself?"

Daniel did. He rose and was taken to the dock. He looked beyond the walls as though surveying the far fells of Cumberland and steadied himself. "I thank the jury for saving me from death, and although I am sorry for the death of Governor Campbell, I did it while this land of ours was in the clutches of Satan. I seemed to be a lone voice. Now I see we fight the Dragon together. Many come forward and I thank them dearly. The killing of the people here must stop and so must the killing of the beasts. For what shall we do when they are all gone? We do not know them. We do not know ourselves. So how can we know them? There's more animal in a man than I ever saw in an animal. We are the children of Cain."

The judge said, "Take him down." And Daniel was taken away with cheering in the court. He looked one last time at Captain Potter. He could see the old sea dog wink and salute. Daniel thought he could even see Potter mouth the words. "All will be well. God is with you." But who could be certain of that?

Doctor Williamson knew he would not live to see his daughter's return from Scotland. Her work had set up systems with the Roslin Institute to start work on the cloning of the Tasmanian tiger wolf. And it might lead to a breakthrough in genetics, almost as great as when Crick and Watson discovered DNA and the secret of life. He was now in possession of the diaries of his great-grandfather, Daniel Williamson, and he had just finished reading again the final entries. He had often wondered about Daniel's first encounter with the tiger wolf in Cumberland and its giant size. Although sad about the struggles of his ancestor, he was proud of his daughter's achievements.

He looked about the shelves of his laboratory at the cub specimens in formaldehyde that he had collected over the decades. He never tired of looking at the skins and samples of extinct species. Ah, why was it that the people who were driven the hardest often lived the longest? That was the case with his great-grandfather, who had passed away at the age of ninety-six. His was the life sentence the most fully served at the old Port Arthur Penitentiary. But then Daniel had been given the chance by the reforming prison governor to devote himself to the animals he loved. He had got his natural family back, just as the Prophet Job, who never lost faith in his God. This was the way for Daniel Williamson. In the end, everything was returned to him. Even the Sinclair knight had come back, as if summoned through time, to defend him against the world. He and his sons founded the veterinary school for prison inmates, which was eventually to become the hub of Tasmanian bio-technical and genetic research.

In his dreams, Doctor Williamson would bring back the lost tiger wolf in its fierce glory. But he would never have imagined that his daughter would be gutsy enough to add to her DNA samples from Tasmania the fur and hide robbed from the ancient stuffed beast of the fells, still kept in the old Keswick Museum. He reopened the press cutting, which he had been sent from England, and found himself almost bristling with pride at the thought of his daughter's tenacity. He pinned the imaginary figure of the Fell boy onto her beautiful form. She was a Williamson, and all. Perhaps she was the brave one. His heart stuttered and he slumped face forward on to the desk. The feeling was curiously peaceful and he felt no fear of what was to come. As the light of the world dimmed, his heart stopped dead. And in his final insight, he saw the tiger wolf back roaming the Cumbrian fells in a flash of fiery might.

EPILOGUE
ROSLIN INSTITUTE, 2008

The beast yawned in its glass cage reinforced by thin steel bars. Its flecked tongue licked the black lips of its huge jaws. Behind its striped body, its tapering tail stretched to a dark point. It could see none of the men in white coats, who fussed around these enclosures of metal and crystal with their syringes and strange speech. The fat sheep in the other pens were too far to reach. The tiger wolf could not pass the invisible walls of its prison.

Then there was the crack of a lock opening. A young woman in a baseball cap, jacket and torn jeans edged through the door. She knew what she was about, and she was well known at the Institute. She came over to the tiger wolf and opened its cage. The beast looked at the young woman. Between them, there was a kind of recognition.

"Come now," the young woman said, "you've been too long in there."

She walked the beast towards the laboratory exit without looking back. It padded after her as quiet as a lurcher. Outside the Pentland hills lay in all their green liberty. The tiger wolf and the young woman loped away.

ABOUT THE AUTHOR

Shawn Williamson has been a merchant seaman on the Great Lakes, the Eastern Seaboard and the North Sea. His interaction with the native people of North America inspired him to study stone-carving on his return to England in the early 80s.

He has since built his reputation as a stone sculptor, with public commissions to his credit in Cumbria and the rest of the UK. He has placed a strong emphasis on community training in all his sculpture projects.

While sculpting a 12-ton Herdwick Ram in the Cumbrian heartlands, he was inspired to write his first novel, *Mauler*. The richness of Scottish and Border history drives his imagination and story-telling ability, a by-product of his ancestral connection with the travelling peoples.